Lion of Ishtar

Book II

Novel

Guido Schenk

Imprint

Bibliografic Information of the German National Library:
The German Library records this publication in the
German National Library; detailed bibliographic data is
available on http://dnb.d-nb.de/

First published in Germany as *Der Löwe der Ischtar* in 2023
Copyright © Guido Schenk 2023
Production and Published: BoD - Books on Demand, Nor-
derstedt, Germany
ISBN: **978-3-75-788160-3**
Translation: Edwin Miles
Cover: Gerhard Junker
Cover Photo: bpk / Vorderasiatisches Museum, SMB /
Olaf M.Teßmer

Contents

Cast of Characters

Akkad – Kingdom of Marduk

Sargon..King of Akkad

Nintinugga...Royal Bodyguard

Gusur................................Eldest Son of King Sargon

Senezon..General (Šagana)

Ezira..General (Šagana)

Subartu – Kingdom of Ishtar

Semiramis...Queen of Subartu

Sanherib.............Captain (Gal-ug) of the Royal Guard

Samše..................................City Governor of Nineveh

Hofileschgu.....................Captain (Gal-ug) of Defense

Woranola.........................Captain (Gal-ug) of Archers

Urta...Leader of the hunters

Nineveh in the Third Millenium BC

VI   Lion of Ishtar

Thirteenth Chapter:
The Holy City

A small group of muskil devoutly climbed the steep steps that led to the sanctuary. Their leader, Nizam-Muskil, led the way. His body was trembling from the exertion of their journey up the mountain. His companions were on the verge of collapse, but he could not take that into consideration. Addad needed to be told about recent events, urgently. In their dust and sweat-caked arms, the muskil carried the insignia of war captured from the Akkadians. Finding new energy, Nizam took the final steps.

On the sanctuary level stood four guards in a line. Nizam nodded to the nearest guard, who was glad to see him back, then trotted inside. The clatter of hooves echoed up the walls, mingling with the hiss of steam rising from the centre of the room and swelling upwards into the sky, where heavy clouds were forming. Soon they would once again hide the land of Subartu from Ishtar's nightly gaze. The goddess had long since been powerless to prevent him from covering her realm. And soon he would wrest it from her completely. The muskil formed a semicircle around the column of steam and dropped to their knees. Patiently, hearts racing, they waited for their god. The hissing grew into a rumble that rose up from the depths of the rocks. The rumbling formed itself into a command: "Speak!" The sanctuary walls shuddered in the presence of the thunder god. The leader of the muskil raised his massive head to speak to the cloud.

"Hail, Addad. We bring the insignia of the Akkadians, as you asked." They held up their spoils, then placed them on the ground in front of them. A satisfied hiss sounded from the cloud.

"Muttakil-Muskil has left for Mari to fetch the chariots. They will arrive in Nineveh at the time you have appointed. All will be done as you have commanded." The steam grew more dense. Dark patches appeared in the white wall, like mighty eyebrows drawn together suspiciously. The thunder god suspected that they had not fully succeeded. Nizam-Muskil swallowed.

"One of our brothers was seen and seriously wounded during the raid on the Akkadians. He succumbed to his injuries. The Akkadians know who seized their insignia." The vapour clouds grew darker. The muskil went on, "Semiramis, queen of Subartu, was in the camp at the time of our raid, staying as a guest. We believe she suspects something of your plans. She has succeeded in persuading King Sargon to lead five hundred of his soldiers to Subartu to protect Nineveh from attack." The rumbling from the cloud grew louder with each sentence the centaur spoke. Lightning flashed in the clouds covering the open roof of the sanctuary, and a thunderous boom shook it to its foundations. Nizam-Muskil, on his knees, swayed. He shouted with all his might to be heard over the noise. "Lord, we tried to stop her, but the witch outsmarted us. We thought we had killed her, but she deceived us with a double. Now she and Sargon have crossed the border and are sailing together to Nineveh."

Again and again, lightning flashed, and thunder roared overhead. The wind howled through the great gates and caused the grim column of vapour to sway menacingly back and forth. Inside it, the muskil thought he could make out a large horned head. Addad himself was only a few steps away. Nizam-Muskil awaited his end. But the rumbling subsided. The lightning stopped and even the cloud gradually started to clear. Addad seemed to be thinking.

After a while, the muskil thought he heard a message from the thunder god inside his head: *It is easy to get people's blood boiling. But they have no patience. We will make them wait until the people weary of them. There is no trust between them. All they seek is their own benefit. The old enmity will soon break out again, and Nineveh will be weaker than ever.*

A rumble thundered from the depths, as if to announce the new mission. New thoughts formed in Nizam-Muskil's mind, like clouds there in the sanctuary: '*Continue your preparations but move half a moon later than originally planned. Until then, let no one see you near the city.* Nizam-Muskil nodded automatically. He had understood. The cloud fell silent. He waited, but he could hear only the wind, which now pushed more gently through the sanctuary and gradually dissipated the clouds. Addad was finished with him. Relieved, the muskil rose to his feet. His head was throbbing from the experience.

But as Nizam-Muskil turned to leave, Addad sent new instructions to his servants. *Round up my bulls! All of them! When the attack takes place, I have a very special task for them.* At that, the rumbling from the depths transformed into a mocking laugh that made the mountain temple shake.

Sargon gazed in wonder at the city, its walls following the river like a long chain of hills, with villages and small docks between the walls and the river. He had never seen such a structure before. The walls had to be twenty metres high, and their rectangular towers reached as high again.

They had passed three great city gates and the stone wall seemed to have no end. The king had heard many stories about the impregnable walls of Nineveh, but he had always dismissed the descriptions as exaggerated. Now he was seeing them with his own eyes. How long had it taken to build these fortifications? Sargon recalled that the expansion of Akkad had taken more than two years, and he had been lucky to face neither a flood nor attack in that time. In the winter after completion, the walls had had to prove themselves for the first time. But Akkad was only about half the size of this city, and its wall seemed to have no end. They had been sailing alongside it for half an hour already. Only at one point was it interrupted, where a channel flowed from the city into the Tigris.

"The Khosr River fills the canals and gardens of Nineveh," Semiramis, beside him, answered his unspoken question. She was proud that he could not take his eyes off her people's structure. "Without it, the city would have to draw its water from the turbulent Tigris, but the space on its banks would not be enough to house all of the people who live here." She had joined him silently and now followed his gaze to the city.

"How many people live in Nineveh?" he asked.

"About forty-eight thousand," the queen answered instantly, as if she'd been expecting the question. "But I really shouldn't be telling an enemy that," she added with a sly smile.

He eyed her in surprise. All of her tension seemed to have fallen away since she had found Nineveh's walls unharmed—she had arrived in time to head off Addad's attack.

Sargon took some time to process the information about the size of Nineveh. His capital, Akkad, was no match for this metropolis. How were they able to feed and organise the masses of people here? The city's administrative apparatus alone must cost a fortune. Then there was the cost of an army and for the maintenance of the walls. Sargon felt an envy of this wealth rising within him.

"Your real enemy already knows," he grumbled, pointing to the mountains visible far beyond the city. Addad ruled there. Dark clouds that hid his realm from the gaze of Ishtar and Marduk gathered around the mountain massif. They towered over the mountain peaks, adding to the already mighty appearance of the weather god's mountain.

After passing the canal mouth, their ships passed a palace complex higher still than the city wall and which reached beyond the city's borders, down to the river itself. Two terraces supported palaces, temples and the houses of the servants and guards. On the top of the upper terrace stood a white temple, to which steep stairs led from all directions. The long shadow of the palace complex reached to the middle of the river, from where the ships from the south were now being directed towards the shore. Another city gate came into view in front of them. The dock in front of it was free of ships, unlike at the previous gates. On the other hand, the shores all around were filled with people. As they approached, Sargon realised that the crowds were there for them. They were expected.

"The captain sent a fast boat ahead the day before yesterday to announce my arrival," Semiramis said. "The city governor, Samše, and her entourage will be there on shore."

"And their soldiers," Senezon added, tightening his helmet.

Indeed, Sargon could see a large unit of armed men on the shore, while archers stood on the battlements of the wall and the city gate. It struck the king that these were the first soldiers he had seen in Nineveh. During the long journey along the city wall, he had not noticed a single guard. Had they been watched in secret? Why bother? Or did the inhabitants of Nineveh rely on the height of their walls? The currents of the Tigris certainly did not permit a surprise attack by day. On the other hand, it would take a very long time for troops in armour to deploy along the walls. The commander in him was thinking now. How many barracks were there along the walls? Certainly at least one on each side of the canal, presumably close to the northern and southern gates. That made the centre the weakest point, he reasoned—if one could speak of weakness at all with such high walls. "You are studying the wrong enemy," Semiramis reminded the men from Akkad. "Please get used to thinking of these soldiers and walls as your allies."

"I hope my new allies are as convinced of their task as you are, Queen Semiramis," Senezon said with a sigh. He was clearly not happy to be within firing range of Nineveh's archers.

"They are," Semiramis replied firmly, ending the conversation. The captain steered the long ship deftly to the dock, where willing hands caught their thrown ropes. They had reached their destination.

Semiramis disembarked first, followed by Sargon and Prince Gusur. The people on the quay fell to their knees as the queen stepped onto solid ground. She went first to the governor, who kissed her hand in greeting and said, "Welcome to Nineveh, Your Majesty! Your presence honours us greatly."

"My heart rejoices to find you in good health. Arise, Samše," the queen replied. The governor did as she was told, keeping a suspicious eye on Sargon as she did so.

"I heard stories about your companions, Your Majesty, but I could not believe—"

"That we have not arrived here in shackles?" asked Sargon before Semiramis could say anything. The numerical superiority of the Subartuan soldiers was also making him nervous.

The stranger's direct address seemed to take the governor a little off guard. She did not answer the Akkadian but instead addressed her words to the queen.

"Your Majesty, we could not believe that you would bring this company to Nineveh. We are a city of peace. We do our best to keep the wars outside our walls."

Semiramis, of course, had noted the conflict between the governor and the king. Sargon suspected that she disapproved of his impulsive reaction.

"And we want to make sure that continues," Semiramis said firmly. "Samše, I present to you Sargon, King of Akkad, Marduk's representative on earth and our ally against the monsters of Addad."

The governor recoiled slightly. Her eyes shifted uncertainly between her queen and the strangers. With forced civility, she said: "I welcome the high lord and his . . . divine assistance. I believe, however, that we do not need to call on his active support in Nineveh.

We live in harmony with Addad and know his monsters only from stories."

"I fear you will soon get to know them better than you would like," Semiramis said. "We know that Nineveh is Addad's next objective to control the worshippers along the Tigris. An attack is imminent." The queen addressed her words less to the governor and more to those around them, who became uneasy.

"An attack by Addad? Your Majesty, you must be mistaken. Who has tried to persuade you of such a thing?"

"His muskil, who tried more than once to kill me on my mission to Akkad," the queen replied. "I have come here to personally organise Nineveh's defences. From now on, the city is under a state of alert! I expect all platoon leaders in the barracks square in one hour to report on mobilisation."

Her words took an officer standing nearby by surprise. She cast a questioning glance at the governor.

"Your Majesty, the city is well prepared at all times," the governor said, avoiding the queen's direct gaze. "Don't you want to move into your residence in the palace? I am happy to have all of the city's gal-ugs assemble there."

"Agreed," said Semiramis, trying her best to stay open to her subordinates' suggestions. "King Sargon and his men will also be staying there."

The governor turned pale. "Your Majesty, do you really want to let these southerners into the city? Would it not be better if they made camp in the field?"

With the rest of the scum you want to keep outside your walls, Sargon thought cynically, but he said nothing.

"King Sargon and his officers will also stay in the palace," Semiramis ordered. "We will find room in the

barracks for his troops—within the walls." She empha-
sised her last words. With that, she strode towards the
gate. The governor had no choice but to follow.

The palace of Nineveh embodied the self-confidence
and pride of its inhabitants. Sargon counted three gates
they had to pass through to reach the innermost city,
each gate larger and more magnificent than the one
before. But apart from the pomp, the complex failed
to impress him. The walls, in his opinion, were far too
close together to be effectively defended, and here, too,
there were few guards to be seen.

The great council chamber surpassed the splendour
of the city gates. Blue bricks covered the walls, brightly
lit by torches. Carved lions, roaring, adorned the rows
of bricks on all sides. Between these walls, decisions
were made that brooked no dissent.

From the centre of the room, a statue of Ishtar,
Nineveh's patron saint, looked down on the new arrivals. Sargon had never seen such a god-figure so large
or majestic before. Marduk was always depicted in re-
lief, surrounded by his servants, and often fighting lions
or bulls. But the statue of Ishtar, leaning against a column, stood almost free in the room. Her slender face
was framed by long, straight hair that fell to her full,
naked bosom. The goddess's arms were raised, lifting
wings across the room, and her open palms were almost
level with her crowned head. Her gesture might have
been a greeting or an attack—Sargon could not be sure
which. The thin wings on the goddess's back were more
like a cloak than the wings of a bird. The goddess's
face quickly captured the observer's eye. It was thin, almost emaciated. *Too gaunt for a goddess of fertility*, Sargon
thought. Her face seemed somehow familiar to him.

Semiramis, who had stepped next to him, gave words to his unspoken thought.

"She has Samše's features," she said.

The governor was standing too far away to hear her words, but she seemed to suspect that the king and queen were talking about the statue, for she stepped closer and explained it to them. "The artist came to Nineveh from the desert. He had not seen any of the statues of our goddess before and carved it based on his observations of her works in the city."

"How did he know which works to ascribe to our heavenly mother?" asked Semiramis.

"The high priestess perfected his vision. She is very pleased with the result."

"Is she?" asked Semiramis slowly, mentally adding Nineveh's high priestess to the list of people she wanted to take a closer look at.

"Extremely pleased," Samše confirmed. But the subject was becoming uncomfortable for her, so she said, "But it is time to hold council, Your Majesty. The gal-ug have assembled."

Sargon eyed the gathering. About twenty women and a few men had gathered in the hall and were kneeling before the queen. The platoon leaders all wore impressive armour made of high-quality metals. In their eyes, however, besides the suspicion that had accompanied him since he had disembarked he saw something else: lethargy. *How can these officers be so listless at a time like this?* he asked himself. Sargon studied their posture more closely. They lacked something that the desert king found even in the youngest of his soldiers: eagerness and readiness for battle. These gal-ug all wore impressive armour, but hardly one among them had a hand on their sword. Sargon was amused to see that one man's sword pommel was caught in his belt. By the time the unfortunate man would be able to draw his weapon, his opponent would have long since cut him in two. Sargon felt that Gusur and his three bodyguards would be more than a match for this group of gal-ug.

But Semiramis had other concerns. "I count only twenty-three gal-ug here," she said to Samše in a voice that carried through the hall. "Nineveh has forty-eight units, each presided over by a gal-ug."

"It used to be that way," Governor Samše admitted. "But as I said, Majesty, Nineveh lives in peace with its neighbours and is protected by impregnable walls. Forty-eight units would be a waste of money."

"Peace is over," Semiramis stated plainly. " I have ordered our troops to mobilise, and I expect to see the other gal-ugs as well."

Samše's eyes widened in horror. "Your Majesty, the troops are urgently needed elsewhere. We are building a new dock to the south of the city right now. The merchants demand that it be finished on time, or they will have to unload at a town further south."

"If we fail to secure Nineveh, the dock won't matter. There will soon be no city left for the traders to call at," the queen replied pointedly. "I expect to see all forty-eight gal-ugs tomorrow at dusk. After that, I want to inspect their soldiers on the parade ground."

"Forty-eight units? Your Majesty, you can't do that!" the governor cried in despair.

"The last time I entered this city, forty-eight units stood guard over me," Semiramis said. Something icy had entered the queen's voice, like a wind blowing from the moon to the earth on a cloudless night. The governor trembled.

"You had the task maintaining the defences of Nineveh, Samše," Semiramis said. "Tomorrow I will know if you are up to it."

The queen turned and left the meeting hall without looking back. Her bodyguard followed close behind. Sargon thought it best to spend the night on the boat and signalled to his followers to go with him. The galugs hurriedly also abandoned the hall, leaving behind a governor gazing in despair at the door through which the queen had disappeared.

The sun grazed the summits of the distant desert mountains as Sargon, Gusur, Ezira and Senezon left the queen's flagship for the parade ground near the northern barracks. Semiramis had sent them a guide to lead them through the maze of city streets, and the Akkadians were grateful for the assistance. Gusur had tried to explore the city on his own during the day, but although the streets of Nineveh were almost deserted in daylight, he had completely lost his orientation. After finally reaching the south gate, he had no desire to venture back into the maze. So he made his way back outside the city, following the city wall. It was faster, but it exposed Gusur to the heat of the day and the glare of the sun. On the way back, he also saw the site of the new dock, so important to the governor. The dimensions of the harbour facility exceeded anything the prince had seen before. It was certainly not something that could be completed at short notice and in a hurry.

With the onset of dawn, life returned to Nineveh. Shops opened their windows, and children came out to play in the streets. While the men marched towards the northern barracks, cows, sheep, and horse-drawn carriages passed them by. Nineveh, as their guide had explained, had two large barracks complexes. The parade ground lay between the northern barracks and the governor's palace. In peacetime—by which he apparently meant the present—only the northern barracks were used to house the soldiers, while the reserve troops stayed with their families either in the city or in the surrounding villages. These "reserves" had now been called up again by Semiramis, which meant that the southern barracks would also soon fill up again.

When they arrived at the parade ground, the Akkadians found it brightly lit by countless torches. The sun had set earlier, but its distant glow still lingered in the sky where the clouds were forming. Over Nineveh, too, Addad was diminishing the influence of the chief deity. As long as Ishtar's stars were in the sky, Addad's clouds kept them out of sight of the world. As well as their relationship to their goddess, Subartu's inhabitants also lost the inspiration of the stars. In the past, it was said that scholars knew how to interpret the position of the stars in pictures and calculate the times of the floods from them. Without the starlight, the people of Subartu had now forgotten that this kind of prediction was possible.

Nineveh's troops had mustered as ordered by their queen. There were exactly forty-eight units with twenty-four troops in each. The gal-ugs—Sargon could not see a man among them today—stood in front of their units. Each gal-ug was armed with a longbow and a short sword, as was the custom in Subartu. The soldiers themselves mostly had only spears and shields. Some also carried a longer sword in their belts, while others were also equipped with the longbow, slung over the shoulder of the bearer along with the arrows. The archers were mainly women. All of the fighters wore long, light-coloured robes held at the waist by a leather belt. Metal helmets, often with long hair flowing from under them, protected the heads of Nineveh's troops. Those with swords also wore breastplates of forged metal. It was an impressive display, and one that only a very wealthy city could afford.

Sargon was offered a seat next to the podium from where he could look over the troops. The queen appeared, followed by Samše and the council elders. Semiramis wore a long white dress that shimmered in the pale light of the moon. The delicate fabric wafted gently in the sweep of her steps, as if woven from clouds that surrounded the queen. Sargon wondered again what art of weaving it was that made the weight of a fabric seem to dissolve to nothing. Semiramis wore a medallion with the seal of the goddess Ishtar on her forehead, the only jewellery that betrayed her royalty. The jewel was held by a thin headband set with precious stones that sparkled like stars.

How different was the governor's outfit. Samše wore a heavy robe similar to the one on the high priest who walked behind her. Long earrings and a massive chain with golden discs framed her narrow face. Her hair was pinned up as if to form a crown and contained more golden discs, all bearing the symbol of Ishtar.

Semiramis strode towards Sargon. More to the following councillors than to him, she said solemnly, "Nineveh's army stands ready. Would the king of Akkad, ambassador of Marduk, join me in the inspection of our troops?"

Sargon did not overlook the dual meaning of "our troops." "We would be honoured to assist the queen of Subartu and daughter of the goddess Ishtar," he replied in the same spirit, and he took the place at her right side, which unmistakably signalled his status as the queen's escort to everyone watching.

Silence had fallen over the parade ground. Only the crackling of the torches and the flags waving in the wind could be heard. Gusur, following his father as usual, unexpectedly found himself in the second row, next to Nineveh's governor. The high priestess was thus forced to join the group behind—she could hardly conceal her indignation at the demotion. She found her place next to Senezon, who followed the prince in rank. Her icy gaze told him what she thought of the presence of the Akkadians. Senezon decided there and then to avoid the priestess and the temple district in Nineveh as far as possible.

Then the inspection demanded his full attention. How many times had he, together with Ezira, mustered the troops for his king, calmed the nervous captains, and reprimanded the soldiers who lacked care or discipline. Now he was among the other side and his experienced eye saw how differently trained the troops presented to them were. The first units were immaculate. Their spears and swords were well cared for, although they bore signs of regular use. The expressions of both men and women were rigid and expressionless, as he expected from fighters who had seen blood and death. These were fighters with whom he could go into battle. Senezon smiled inwardly. He, too, had put his elite soldiers at the start of an inspection, to put the king in a good frame of mind.

But the longer they walked the lines of guards, the more markedly the quality of Nineveh's fighters also diminished—to a degree that took Senezon's breath away. He would never have dared to present such a slipshod crew to his king. Sometimes it was a missing breastplate, sometimes a bored expression or an impatient movement of the hands that revealed a soldier's lack of discipline. Some, it almost seemed to him, were wearing armour for the very first time. More than once, Senezon wondered if the bearer of a spear had ever actually thrown it. Some of the soldiers were too young, others clearly too old for the rigours of a long battle. There were even a number of wounded women in the ranks. The quality of the troops improved again somewhat at the end, as if to make a good last impression. Senezon knew that such tricks would not go unnoticed by his king.

The governor, who marched along the ranks beside Prince Gusur, took no notice of military details. She was basking in her success at having raised twenty-five new units in less than twenty-four hours. She had even found old armour and weapons for them, and almost all of the soldiers were properly equipped.

Senezon, on the other hand, alternated between indignation and outright scorn. This was a particularly poor gathering of soldiers. Some time ago, Akkad's spies had reported to him that Nineveh's military strength was not good, and still the sight of this bunch came as a shock. In peacetime, such soldiers could do no more than police a market square. Nineveh had little more to set against a serious attack than the thick walls behind which its soldiers hid.

On their journey to Subartu, Senezon had regarded Queen Semiramis's bodyguard with respect, but the lamentable guards of Nineveh did little to affirm his esteem for Subartu's military strength. He did the maths: one thousand one hundred and fifty soldiers had lined up, about half of whom he considered serviceable. A quarter could function as reserves with a little training.

The rest were useless. So together with the troops from Akkad, there were now about one thousand decent soldiers in Nineveh. The greatest protective contribution would come from the walls and defensive weapons. The size of the city meant that it would take a long time to move troops from one part of the city to another, so they had to prevent a surprise attack.

After they had finished the inspection and returned to the podium, the governor could no longer restrain her impatience and proudly said, "You see, Your Majesty? Just as you ordered. Forty-eight units ready to defend Nineveh."

Semiramis eyed her coolly and chose her words carefully. "Forty-eight units I see. However, with regard to their operational readiness, I have a different opinion." Sargon nodded in agreement, but this time refrained from commenting. The governor was visibly shocked. "Not ready? You can see they are all carrying weapons. They're just waiting to use them bravely against our enemies." At this she glanced at Sargon, as if to show whom she considered an enemy of the city.

"Then we shouldn't keep such brave fighters waiting," Senezon murmured, but loud enough to be heard on the podium. King Sargon nodded to him. The general gestured to Ezira and Gusur to follow him and the three companions strode into the ranks of soldiers. About halfway in, Senezon approached a unit leader who had caught his eye earlier when he was inspecting the troops. She was about twenty years old, wore her long blonde hair down her back and held her nose a little higher than those around her.

"I am Senezon, son of Enmetena and šagana of the First Army of Akkad. What is your name?"

"I am Mishumi, daughter of Anyun, leader of Group Five North," the woman replied proudly.

"Now, Mishumi, daughter of Anyun, leader of Group Five North, we want to prove your fortitude to Queen Semiramis. Instruct three of your soldiers to challenge me." The woman cast a questioning glance towards Semiramis, who indicated with a gesture that this was also her command. Mishumi chose two women and one man from her unit and stood them in front of Senezon and his companions.

"You misunderstood me," Senezon said. "These three are for me." Before the young woman could respond, Ezira stepped forward and called for challengers as well. Gusur followed his example. Puzzled, Mishumi assigned three opponents to each of them. Semiramis suspected that, despite their superior numbers, Nineveh's soldiers would be no match for Akkad's fighters. And as much as the demonstration was necessary to rouse the troops, she wanted to avoid unnecessary bloodshed.

"Take spears without tips. Anyone who touches the ground with their hand or any other part of their body above the knees is eliminated," she stipulated.

The three Akkadians duly laid down their weapons. Each took one of the prepared practise spears. Their opponents followed suit and surrounded the Akkadians, who formed a triangle with their backs to each other. They stood close enough to give cover, but not so close as not to hinder each other.

The signal to start the battle rang out. Nineveh's nine soldiers surrounded their opponents, looking for a point to attack. Gusur made a leap forward, feigning an attack, and two of the soldiers immediately struck at him. Their action, however, was not coordinated.

Both tried to strike him in the chest. Gusur knocked both blows aside with his spear and used his momentum to stab one of his adversaries in the stomach with the other end. The stricken man sank to his knees with a groan. At the same time, Gusur kicked the other man in the face, knocking him out. Before more blows could come down on him, he was already back position. Senezon nodded appreciatively to the prince.

Yelling angrily, Nineveh's remaining combatants struck at the trio. But for all their shouting, their attacks made little impression. Their advances were too predictable. The Akkadians, on the other hand, formed a cohesive unit. Each had not only his direct adversaries in view, but also his comrades, and their triangle remained unbroken. Their attackers did not cover each other—every strike opened a gap to counterattack. And Sargon's men knew how to use the gaps. One by one, through missteps and carelessness, their opponents' numbers dropped. When the three Akkadians were left facing only two adversaries, Semiramis brought the fight to an end.

"Enough!" she called loudly. The combatants stopped and bowed to each other. A shocked silence fell over the parade ground.

"Warriors of Nineveh," she continued, "a storm is gathering that threatens to engulf our city. After years Addad of plundering our fields and merchants, Addad now lusts after Nineveh itself." She stepped down from the podium and paced among the troops again. "He has waited a long time, has taken from us Ishtar's gaze, and has cut the safe routes between our cities. We thought our enemies were in Akkad, and all the while he prepared his army in the mountains and struck when our troops returned weakened from battle."

"For many years we believed that Addad had allied himself with Marduk to destroy Ishtar and us. We were deceived. Addad does not share. With my own eyes, I have seen his storms fall upon the armies of Akkad. I have seen how his clouds robbed the people of Marduk's gaze in daylight. His bulls find easy prey in the villages that are not protected by high walls like our cities."

She reached the place where Gusur, Senezon, and Ezira were standing.

"You have seen for yourselves just how impressively the Akkadians can fight. Spear and shield are powerful weapons in the hands of skilled men and women. But even more so is the unity shared by the fighters, a unity forged in many battles. Could have stood up to a force of such fighters if they had invaded our land? Is that what you think?

"We know about Marduk's futile attempts to lead his troops into our land. Ishtar stood by us, but the decisive moment only came when Addad intervened. Sore and beaten, the attackers were forced to retreat, and we too suffered losses. In all our battles, the only victor has ever been the god of thunder.

"Addad has got used to winning. He is now strong enough to bring his troops from the mountains to the rivers and overrun our cities. But he has made a mistake. He has underestimated the wisdom of our goddess and Marduk. We know his plan and together we will stop him here. Here, at the gates of Nineveh." She pointed to the Akkadians. "These men do not come as conquerors. They come to help us weather the storm. They will teach you the fighting skills you have just observed. Marduk trusts you to use them against your true enemies."

There is no turning back now, Semiramis thought. *I hope the city leaders also appreciate their help.* Sargon seemed to be thinking the same. Together they watched the close inspection of the troops that followed, during which Ezira and Senezon took notes for the briefings they had promised in their announcement. After an hour, the soldiers were sent back to their posts. The gal-ugs remained before the podium while the city councillors withdrew. Governor Samše, as representative of the city's military leadership, stayed as well, as did Sargon and his men, to plan their defensive preparations.

Semiramis turned to Samše. "Besides our troops, our walls and defensive weapons will decide the battle. I want to see all our available weaponry at this time tomorrow, and I want to inspect the walls, as well." The governor seemed to be inwardly resisting another day of hasty preparation but said nothing.

"How do you intend to train our troops, King Sargon?" Semiramis asked the Akkadian. Sargon took notice of her formal tone of voice and chose his words carefully.

"We can train in close combat with about half of them. The other half should practise with bows and the defensive weapons." He handed her the clay tablet with the allocation of the units.

"If a real army actually attacks, we will need more troops for close combat," Samše cut in. "If the walls are breached, the archers will be defenceless. You should share your knowledge with all of Nineveh's soldiers."

"It would not help them," Sargon replied. "Knowledge isn't enough. It also takes physical strength and the will to thrust a sword into an enemy's body. That can only be trained in battle."

Semiramis was worried about the low strength of their ground forces. "How many field units will you be able to assemble?" she asked.

"Three. And the Akkadians will work alongside your troops in each of them. Gusur, Ezira and Senezon will each lead a unit."

"Men as leaders?" said Samše in amazement.

Sargon looked sternly at the governor. Only with difficulty did he suppress a rebuff. After a deep breath, he said, "Governor, I am aware that it is unusual in Subartu to put men in charge. We have had good experience with this, and I think these three have also gained the respect of your troops today."

"Respect for their strength and combat skills, yes, but leading troops requires other qualities. You men are far too stubborn for that," the governor replied spiritedly.

That was too much for Semiramis. She would not have this discussion in the presence of the gal-ugs. "Extraordinary circumstances call for extraordinary measures. I have come to know all three officers and trust them as leaders. They do not have the knowledge of our šaganas, of course, but why should they not learn from each other?" With that, the subject was closed.

"Do you have riders in the city that can act as scouts?" Sargon asked the governor.

"Horses are very expensive," the governor replied. "We use horsemen only as couriers."

"Then we should also set up scout units to warn us of an attack in time." He turned to Semiramis. "Addad will approach from the mountains north or east. If we focus on those directions, two detachments should do."

"Agreed," decided the queen. "You are men of the desert. I will leave the selection and training of the scouts to you."

Samše could see the costs of Nineveh's armies swelling rapidly. "Your Majesty, you yourself have noted that we will not have enough troops to withstand a ground attack. Creating new detachments will not help that. We should look more to the formation of a standing army."

Semiramis gave Sargon a questioning look, and he replied with a barely noticeable shake of his head. He did not want to inform the governor about the support of Enna-Dagan's troops. Not yet. And there was more help to be had, after all. To the governor, Semiramis said, "I agree with you that we need more ground troops, but I also agree with King Sargon that we will not find them in Nineveh. I will therefore send a messenger to the city of Nemrik to request more units from there."

The city governor tried once again to change her queen's mind. "Your Majesty, we have lived at peace with Addad for many years. He has never attacked our villages and there is no suggestion that he will do so soon. I understand your wish to see that the city can defend itself, and I am grateful for the assistance rendered by the exalted king of Akkad. But that should be enough."

Semiramis was beginning to lose her patience. Had the governor not understood that she would tolerate no discussion on this issue, even less so in the presence of subordinates? The governor had clearly been able to rule unchecked for too long, to the point where she found it difficult to submit even to her queen. Another sign was needed. Coldly, she replied, "Governor Samše, I think it would be to everyone's advantage for you to leave this concern to those more versed in military matters and to concentrate on supplying the troops and the people of the city." She turned demonstratively to Sargon. "King Sargon, ruler of Akkad, representative of Marduk, it is my wish that you take command of all the troops of Nineveh, those present and those yet to come." A murmur rose among the gal-ugs. A stranger—a man at that—was to lead them?

Sargon bowed low before the queen and replied, "Queen Semiramis does me a great honour. Your wish shall be done. From now on, let us speak no more of the origins of our soldiers. We are the defenders of Nineveh and her queen." He turned to the leaders and raised his sword in a battle cry. "For Nineveh!"

The platoon leaders were stunned at first. But then they too raised their weapons and shouted, "For Nineveh!" Then they shouted it again, and this time Gusur, Senezon, and Ezira joined in. The king had them shout it a third time, the battle cry ringing far into the city.

Samše was trembling with fury. The queen had offered not a single word of praise for her work to restore the troops so quickly. And then she had had to listen to the Akkadians, who were permitted to doubt the readiness of Nineveh's troops in front of everyone. In her eyes, the entire exercise was not only a waste of time but also took valuable manpower from other projects. Not only did Samše have to swallow the higher costs for the army, but she had also been relieved of her command over the troops. Queen Semiramis, she felt, was pulling the rug from under her feet. But all was not yet lost. The city council and the temple were still under her control. Those were the real sources of power over Nineveh, and through them she would also get her soldiers back.

She followed the queen back to the palace, while King Sargon marched to the barracks with his newly acquired troops.

Fourteenth Chapter:
Building the Defenses

Semiramis completed her message to the Nemrik council by imprinting her seal. It would take a fast messenger four days to reach the city, and then it would take time to raise the troops and send them back to Nineveh. They could expect help in two weeks at the earliest. The queen let the clay tablet bake over the brazier to make sure the signs would not become blurred on the journey. Then she stepped out into the antechamber, where the messenger and the city council were waiting for her.

"This is my message to Issar-duri, governor of Nemrik. Keep it safe. You are to give it only to her, or to her successor, should anything happen to Issar-duri." Then she took an amulet and placed it around the young woman's neck. "You are now a messenger for the goddess Ishtar. Everyone in our realm is obliged to help you. Anyone who stops or hinders does so at the cost of their life. Travel fast and rest only during the greatest heat of the day. You will be given a fresh horse and lodging wherever you knock. The future of Nineveh depends on the success of your mission."

The messenger bowed low, thanked the queen for her trust, and left the palace. A horse was already waiting for her outside the gates.

Samše glanced questioningly at one of her servants. She nodded. She too had completed her preparations.

When the queen withdrew to compose her message to the city of Nemrik, Samše had secretly summoned three men from her personal guard.

"A messenger will leave shortly for Nemrik from the west gate. She will have a horse from the stables and will be taking the road along the Tigris to the north. At the crossroads that turns off to Chorsabad is a village. She will take her first rest there. She must not reach the village."

The men nodded. They had sworn allegiance to their governor, to the death. could trust them blindly. "Should we silence her permanently?" one asked.

Samše shook her head. "It will be enough to hold her prisoner until I have convinced Her Majesty that this request for troops is entirely unnecessary. In Chorsabad, seek out a merchant named Shimmokeen. Give him this pouch and he will keep the messenger and her horse safe."

"Where do we get horses?"

Samše pointed to one of her servants. "Shashank will show you a place at the Nergal gate, where you will also be equipped. And you will report to me as soon as you return. Do your job well and you will be well rewarded." The men bowed and followed the servant out. Moments later, another servant appeared and reported that the queen had dined and was now calling for writing materials for her message. Satisfied that she had regained some power over her own destiny, the governor gave instructions accordingly.

"The huts are just piles of rubble," Gusur exclaimed as he inspected the southern barracks with his father. Numerous roofs had fallen in, and doors and shutters were missing or standing open. Goats, chickens, and sheep grazed on the abandoned parade ground, which was overgrown with bushes and grass.

Sargon frowned. "These barracks must have been empty for at least a year," he said. "Semiramis hasn't been in Nineveh for three years. At that time, she told me, both barracks were immaculately maintained."

"And this is where we're supposed to live?" asked Gusur. "We'd rather stay on board the ship."

"It's certainly more hospitable there than here," the king replied patiently. "But if there's an attack, we'd be cut off by the enemy before we even made it to the walls."

"And if we camp in the open? We could set up camp between the town and the path to the mountains. From there we can send out the scouts and retreat to the city in time if Addad's forces advance."

"That would do," Sargon admitted. "But you forget that we are now with Nineveh's troops. Either we stay in the barracks together or drive a wedge between us and them forever."

Prince Gusur gave it up. When the king set his mind on something, it was hard to change his mind. "Then at least we'll be around when they have to get their noble hands dirty," the young man said, alluding to the ornamented hands of the female leaders, which he had noticed during their inspection. Their fingernails were long and shapely—Gusur could not recall seeing anything like it in Akkad. But fingernails were impractical for manual work or if you had to wield a sword. And while the women among Nineveh's troops wore no jewellery, the backs of their hands were often ornately decorated and emanated a certain promise. Gusur felt a stirring between his legs when he thought of it.

"I don't think fixing the barracks makes the best use of our soldiers," his father said, bringing the young man's thoughts back to earth. "The city must have slaves and craftsmen who can do that for us. We need to focus on training and preparing for the attack."

He had the scribe who accompanied them take notes about this—later, they would present them to the city council. They calculated the division of the units among the buildings, allowing for separate barracks for men and women, each with its own bathrooms and a fireplace. There was also an alcove for an altar in each house. Gusur wondered if what Marduk would think about his fighters sleeping in a barracks with an altar dedicated to Ishtar. He decided to have a sacrificial site dedicated to Marduk built at the parade ground. The god should see how they proved themselves worthy of him.

"We'll run the combat troop drills in the northern barracks," Sargon specified. "Most of them are already housed there, anyway. The parade ground at the south barracks will be for spear training, archery, and the defensive machines."

"And riders?" asked Gusur.

"Nineveh does not keep many horses, as you heard. Besides, the streets offer no room for chariots. Our battle will take place on the walls. When they break, we'll be fighting hand-to-hand in the streets and buildings."

"But our scouts need to be on horseback."

His father nodded. "For selection and training, we'll need space that isn't available in the city. Let's take a look at the field you suggested in the north. It might be the right place for that."

An idea came to Gusur. "How are you going to break us up for the training?" he asked cautiously.

The king seemed well aware of what his son was thinking and laughed heartily. "So moving in here be worth it for those beautiful hands, would it?"

Gusur blushed. He thought it best not to say anything back.

"Don't worry, my boy, Ezira is the most experienced spearman of all of you. I would prefer to have Nintinugga here to lead the archers, but we will find someone from Nineveh. They seem to know a lot about that already. Senezon has already put himself forward for sword fighting, so I'll leave the training of the scouts in your hands."

Relieved, Gusur knelt before his father. "Thank you, Father. I will not betray your trust."

"I know that already," Sargon spoke. "But be warned. I have yet to see a soldier here on horseback. Nor are you likely to find riders already trained to fight. You will have to teach them all of it."

"They will make you proud, I swear it," Gusur said.

"I hope so. Whether we can hold the walls will depend on them. Time in this city is not on our side."

Semiramis, with Samše beside her, was already waiting for Sargon when he arrived at the Nergal Gate, in the north of the city, to inspect the walls and defences. The queen was wearing a simple, light-blue robe, similar to her soldiers' uniforms but of far finer fabric. Her belt was not made of leather but had been braided from shimmering ribbons. The robe reached to just above her knees—Sargon could see her pale legs and feet, on which she wore fine sandals studded with precious stones. She did not appear to be carrying weapons, but he had no doubt her robe had hidden pockets for them. He relayed to the queen his observations in the southern barracks and how he had set up the training of the troops.

Semiramis took the scribe's notes and passed them to the governor. "Make sure our troops don't have to work on repairs to the barracks. We need them ready when Addad's troops are at the walls."

If that day ever comes, the governor thought. Aloud, however, she asked, "What will happen to the jetty at the south gate? The soldiers were always when it came to anchoring the piles and securing the site."

"We'll see tomorrow which soldiers we want to keep and who we'll be sending home again," Sargon replied. "I'm sure you'll find many among them who are willing to work on the barracks or building your jetty."

Samše knew perfectly well that the rejects would be of little use in construction work. Her queen raised no objections to Sargon's suggestion, and Samše had to submit to her fate. *Patience,* she thought to herself. The *time will come when I can prove to our queen the futility of all your training and drills.*

Semiramis introduced Sargon to a woman in her entourage. "This is Hofileshgu, daughter of Totosa. She oversees the city's defences." The woman bowed deeply to Sargon, as appropriate when greeting a superior officer. Her look was confident and wary, but not aggressive. She wore a plain tunic held by a sturdy leather belt that held tools and a long-bladed knife. The muscles of her arms and legs were well-crafted and her skin was darker than that of the gal-ugs presented to the king on the parade ground. Sargon acknowledged her bow with a slight nod.

"Hofileshgu has held this position for over ten years," Semiramis continued. "She knows the walls and also the fields outside the city. I cannot think of a better person to command our defensive machines." The king had no immediate objections, although he did not know exactly what defensive machines she was talking about. He had been preoccupied with another question since his survey of the southern barracks.

"It is important that your machines and the archers act as one. Who would you suggest to lead the archers?" The woman seemed surprised that the King of Akkad would turn to her for such an important question. Before daring to answer, she quickly cast a glance at the queen, who replied with a nod of approval. She was pleased to see that Sargon did not want only his men to fill the officer positions.

"Woranola, daughter of Quichoka, leads the second unit north. She is a sure shot and has the gift of conveying her self-assurance to other archers as well." Queen Semiramis had no objection to her choice, and Woranola was summoned to join the inspection.

"Our biggest challenge is to secure the eastern wall," explained Hofileshgu as they walked along the wall. "At twenty thousand cubits, it is the longest of the four walls and lacks the protection of a river. About a thousand cubits east, the plain rises to a hill that we cannot see beyond even from our watchtowers."

"Siege catapults aren't likely to reach the city from there, are they?" Sargon asked.

"No. If they could, we would have had the hill removed long ago," the woman replied somewhat pointedly, as if stating the obvious. Sargon knew that an undertaking of that magnitude was anything but commonplace, even with Nineveh's achievements, but he let her have her way.

"We have three gates north of the Khosr and three south along the eastern wall," the woman continued. "The gates in the southern part are further apart, so each has its own assigned unit. In the northern section, two units are enough to secure the three gates."

Sargon was not convinced that such thinly spread troops could provide sufficient resistance in case of attack, but his doubts were eased when he realised that the towers stored enough spears and arrows to supply many times that number. Overall, the impeccable condition of the walls and the arrangement of the towers reduced his concerns about the city's defences. "I've heard mention several times of machines you use for defence," he said, turning to Hofileshgu. "What's this all about?"

He had obviously chosen a topic that the woman had been waiting for. Her eyes sparkled with pride, and she said, "Follow me, King Sargon. You will see with your own eyes that no army in the world can breach our walls."

Halfway between two gates, they came to a platform that supported a wooden scaffold on a pivot. Mighty poles supported a wooden spar, at the end of which was a woven basket held tightly in place by strong straps. The men and women working at the machine stood up when they saw the group approaching. "Show the king how we defend our city!" Hofileshgu said.

The crew quickly heaved a heavy stone into the basket. One came to Hofileshgu and asked, "What is the target, Ma'am?" She pointed to a patch of scrub about six hundred cubits from the wall, and the man bowed and made some adjustments to the machine.

Strong arms turned the platform until the machine was pointing in the desired direction. Hofileshgu asked the onlookers to step up to the wall and watch the defensive action from there. Then the leader shouted an order and a man cut a strap that anchored the basket to the ground. The spar shot up, pulled by the straps, until it crashed loudly against a beam across the top of the machine. The stone flew in a high arc overhead and came down directly on top of the bushes that the leader had chosen as her target. Dust swirled as the stone crashed into the earth.

Sargon was impressed. With this, the city could take out not only troops, but entire siege towers in a single blow. And without siege towers, no attackers would be able to reach the battlements or break down the walls. He took a close look at the machine and then snapped an order: "Reset the machine!"
Hofileshgu seemed to realise what the king was getting at, and she urged the catapult crew to hurry. Nevertheless, it was a long time before the basket, after a few failed attempts, was secured by a new strap and again in position to receive the next stone.

Semiramis had also recognised the weakness of this wonderful machine. "You have only one shot," she concluded. "A siege tower would be at the wall before you could use it a second time."

Hofileshgu admitted that this was true, but objected, "A siege tower is an easy target. It is much bigger than a bush and moves very slowly."

"That may be. But an attacker will set up more than one siege tower to take the walls of Nineveh."

"Where are the other machines?" asked Sargon.

"We set them up in the middle, between the gates. Each platform can also be rotated so that neighbouring machines can support each other."

"That will stop the attackers, but not forever. The archers and lancers have stopped the second wave. If even one tower gets through, Nineveh is lost."

"In our lifetime, no siege tower has ever succeeded in breaking through our defences. We will repel any attack," replied the governor, pre-empting her gal-ug.

"Let us pray to Ishtar that your prophecy comes true," Semiramis said, to which Sargon added, "And may our troops prepare together from now on, also to ensure its fulfilment."

The messenger from Nineveh patted her horse lightly on the neck. "Come on," she said softly to the animal. "We'll be there soon. Just a few more miles to the village of the happy fishermen. You can rest there." . . . *while I ride on*, she completed the sentence in her mind. She knew the area north of Nineveh well.

Her progress so far had been slow. Traders with their wagons, flocks of sheep, soldiers, even simple hikers were making their way north. The roads only emptied when the sun rose and the day grew hot. Then she was able to make better speed. The horse was a strong, brown stallion, powerfully built and with great stamina, a regal animal that only a few were privileged to ride. The messenger enjoyed the feeling of flying along the roads on his back, leaving everything behind. She thanked the goddess more than once for this grace.

Behind a bend in the road, she came across a small group of travellers. Three horses were standing at the side of the road. One of the travellers was waving fiercely while another knelt beside a body on the ground. A fall. The messenger reined in her horse as she approached the spot.

She heard the man call to her while she was still quite far: "Please help! My companion has fallen badly, and we are strangers here." She slowed the horse to a walk as she drew closer.

"Don't worry," she said to him as she approached. "There is a village near here known for its hospitality. You will be treated well there." She brought her horse to a halt beside the man. He was tall and muscular. *Almost like a soldier*, she thought. *But without armour.* He carried a short knife in his belt.

The man eyed the messenger carefully. His gaze lingered on the amulet she wore around her neck. He said: "Thank you. Then our companion is saved. You seem to know this area. Is there an inn nearby? We will gladly pay for your stay there as well."

"I'm afraid that is impossible. I'm on urgent business in the service of Ishtar. But you will have no trouble finding the inn. It is right at the start of the village."

In the meantime, the second man had joined them, and they now stood on either side of the messenger. "Our friend needs a stretcher," the second man said. "If you and your horse will help, I can ride ahead and get everything prepared. Please help us!"

"I'm sorry," the woman said, "but my assignment can't wait."

"Yes, it can," the second man said in a firm voice, and he took hold of the horse's bridle. His well-built companion drew his knife. "Things will go better for you, girl, if you dismount now." She looked at the man in horror. Then, with all her might, she kicked him in the face. He sprawled on the ground, dropping the reins, and she jerked them back without hesitation. The stallion reared up, forcing the second man to throw himself to the ground to avoid the hooves. That was enough. The way ahead was clear again and she spurred her horse forward. She did not see the arrow that bored into her back and sent her tumbling down. Her horse ran on, now riderless.

The muscular man had jumped to his feet, grabbed his bow, and sent the arrow after her.

"Idiot!" his accomplice growled, rubbing his face, which was swollen from the kick. "The governor wanted her kept alive."

"You're the idiot," the third man snapped, also on his feet again. "You had her horse by the reins, and she fooled you like a raw recruit."

"We could still have caught up and captured her," his accomplice defended himself.

"Yeah? The village starts just behind the next bend. Even if we caught up, she'd be screaming for help. She knows the area, have you forgotten?"

The other man fell into a sullen silence. There was nothing to be done about it now. "What do we do now?" he asked when they reached the body. The young woman had broken her neck in the fall and died instantly. The arrow was still in her back and blood was seeping from the wound.

"We get her off the road and bury her under stones before anyone else comes along."

"Shouldn't we burn her?"

"Too dangerous. The smoke would blow into the village and people might get curious."

A depression in the ground not far from the road offered a suitable place to hide the girl's corpse. While his companions covered her limp body with stones and sand, the leader covered their tracks and the blood left on the road. When they were finished, they looked at their work with satisfaction. No one would guess there was a body under the stones. The muscular man took out the pouch he'd received from the governor, and all three eyed the silver it contained greedily.

"The merchant won't be needing this now," he decided. "All we have to do is keep our mouths shut."

"What do we say?"

"We intercepted the messenger as ordered and handed her over to the merchant. When our mistress summons him, he'll deny everything, of course. But what can he prove? There's one of him and three of us. She'll think he killed her to save himself the trouble."

The others agreed. It was a simple plan. They split the spoils three ways.

"Before we return to Nineveh, we should spend a few days in Nemrik," the leader decided. He wanted his companions to spend their silver there rather than in Nineveh. Sudden wealth would attract unwanted attention at home. The others agreed and all three rode north to the city.

"And again! Shield and thrust, shield and thrust!" The men and women of the units sweated as they executed the formation again and again. Senezon sighed. *Lone wolves, all of them.* He'd been watching them closely. Some were barely able to wield a sword for more than half an hour, others were too impatient to maintain the discipline of a unit. He had already sent five home that day because they were unsuitable for the army. *Who hires such soldiers?* he wondered in despair.

He looked to the other end of the square, where Ezira was training his spearmen. The two generals had agreed to work with both the spearmen and the swordsmen on the grounds in the northern part of the city. The parade ground at the southern barracks was in a pitiful state and, for now, could only be used for training in ranged combat.

King Sargon had agreed to the plan reluctantly. None of the Akkadian officers were at the manoeuvres in the south, and he was not happy about that. Finally, however, they had convinced him that Hofileshgu had the most experience with ranged weapons. He had also been impressed by the gal-ug's knowledge and conduct. The king had made it is habit to entrust competent officers with important responsibilities.

If Addad succeeded in entering the city with his cavalry, they would need a phalanx of long spears to repel them. Without the spears, Senezon's swordsmen would simply be mown down, so Ezira had his spear-carrying troops practising close combat with their weapons. Senezon turned his attention back to his own units. There were repeated incidents where soldiers did not hold the line and instead jumped into an attack overzealously. This time it was a young man with long arms—and his impetuous attack did not escape Senezon for a second. He shouted angrily, "You! Why are you jumping out of line? Are you so eager to die young?"

The man looked at him grimly but said nothing. He stepped back into the line. A new round began.

They had been training for three days and nights. The citizens of Nineveh rested during the day and the troops only trained when the sun had set. Senezon was used to the rhythm, although he was annoyed at not being able to stand beneath Marduk's sun. The clear, warming rays had always been like a master's hand on his shoulder, admonishing when he was careless, encouraging when his task felt too great. The clouds of

Addad had dimmed the light in recent years, but the glow had never completely disappeared. In the land of the northern queen, he had rediscovered the full glow of the day with joy, like a long-lost friend. *By Marduk! What a pity I can't drill these sleepyheads in your light,* the broad-shouldered fighter thought. But that would be asking too much of the people of Subartu, who fled from the daylight as if it would burn them.

At night, the power of Addad's mountainous clouds was far greater than during the day. The position of the moon could only be guessed, and the stars were almost never visible. Senezon didn't care. *Dark is dark,* was all he thought. As long as the clouds did not come so low as to obscure the view at ground level, it made no difference which god denied him Marduk's light. *Let them settle their squabbles and let me go back to my homeland.*

A shout brought him back to the present. A soldier had fallen, taking the man next to him to the ground as well. Senezon was instantly on top of them, ranting at both of them.

"That is what I'm trying to explain to you. It's not enough that you heroes keep your eyes on your enemy. You have to pay attention to your unit, too, especially the man next to you—or the woman." The gal-ugs from Subartu were very sensitive about gender.

"That's it for you. Units seven, eight, nine and ten north, fall in!" he bellowed across the square. The soldiers had been drilling for hours and were practically dead on their feet. Medics rushed to tend to those who were struggling the most. Word had spread quickly that the general was hard on his troops, and by the second night a healer and her servants had already set up camp near the parade ground. The skill with which she treated the exhausted soldiers impressed Senezon, who had seen his share of battles. Sometimes she wrapped herbs into her bandages, sometimes she gave the bruised and beaten patient something to drink or simply pressed her hands firmly against the damaged area of their body. It wasn't long before the patient had recovered, or at least felt well enough to take part in the next exercise. Senezon resolved, on his return home, to find someone like her to attend his troops' training and exercises.

"Seventeen injured! In three nights!" Governor Samše shrilled. Her voice echoed off the wood-panelled walls of the council chamber, at the front of which the over-sized statue of Ishtar gazed down on those present. Semiramis sat on a raised throne in front of the statue, her back to the goddess. A chair had also been fashioned for the king of Akkad and placed at her side, but Sargon rarely stayed in it for long. He was standing at a table with clay tablets that recorded the troops' provisioning. The stock of spearheads and shields in the city was far too low for the troop strength they were trying to build for the defence. Nineveh's merchants had quickly recognised the opportunities on offer and were outbidding each other to supply the royal troops.

Manoeuvres had already begun, and Ezira and Senezon reported to him every morning on their progress with the soldiers. *Overall, things were coming along passably,* he was thinking, before the governor stormed into the chamber in a rage. Practically shaking with anger, she held up a clay tablet. Apparently she had her own sources within the army, possibly even among the platoon leaders. The king decided to warn Senezon as soon at the next opportunity.

"A pregnant woman suffered a shock and almost lost her baby!" the governor continued. "I cannot allow the citizens of this city to be treated like this."

Sargon saw fit to object: "Senezon is an experienced general. I have full confidence in his methods," he stated simply.

"The methods of a cattle herder," she railed back.

"Governor!" Semiramis stepped in, trying to mediate in the dispute. "King Sargon and I are pleased to see that you are also paying attention to military issues, although I know your time is limited. Why don't you share your concerns you and how we might improve our preparations? We are always open to suggestions." With this she signalled that Samše's concerns were being taken seriously, but also that the governor was not to interfere in military matters. The governor understood the message well, but she did not give up easily.

"I have been told by several high-ranking members within our forces that drills and exercises have dragged on for hours without a break. Some of our soldiers collapsed from exhaustion during the sword fighting and were dragged back to their feet and forced to continue. And the šagana is quick to use the stick if someone does not do as he says as quickly as he deems fit. The man completely lacks the empathy a responsible leader needs. You cannot treat people like animals."

Sargon felt it necessary to defend his general. "Senezon has been training soldiers for more than ten years. Discipline is the backbone of any troop. Without it, your skills are useless. I understand your concern for the servicemen," he said, endeavouring to respond to the governor's concerns "and women," he added quickly when he saw her anger. "I am confident our troops will be in top shape."

"And I am confident we will have no one left if we actually are attacked," the governor snapped back. "We have suffered more casualties from a day of your manoeuvres than in a year of normal service. Do you mean to abandon our city entirely to the Akkadians?" She addressed her question directly to Semiramis.

So that's what you're up to, Sargon thought. *You want me to subordinate my troops to your followers. Then there'll be an "unfortunate misunderstanding" or two, and we'll feel compelled to leave. The woman's tough,* Sargon had to admit.

Semiramis looked on as the two disparate characters locked horns. Sargon fought with the barely restrained energy of the desert wind and Samše with the fluidity and pressure of water. And the longer their fight lasted, the greater the governor's chances of winning became.

Semiramis put an end to it. "We have charged King Sargon and his šaganas with the defence of Nineveh because we consider them the best for the job. Their instructions to our troops are mine," she said, immediately reconfirming the order of precedence. "At the same time, we are well aware that we are only human. People make mistakes and we should learn from many perspectives. Please continue to share your concerns with me, Governor. I value your suggestions."

On the surface, the governor showed disappointment at not having achieved more. She bowed deeply and left the hall. But Samše's success was not lost on Sargon. Semiramis had opened the door for the governor to speak to her in confidence, without the desert king's presence. Frowning, he said, "If civilians are training Nineveh's military, then I'm beginning to understand why your troops are in such a sorry state."

Semiramis looked at the king. "These are brave men and women who serve Nineveh and me," she said, hurt. "They may be unpractised, but they give their all for their city."

Sargon nodded towards the door through which the governor had disappeared. "I don't doubt their willingness to sacrifice, Semiramis. But without coordination, without discipline, they will end as Addad's tragic victims, no more." He stepped towards her. "I talked to Ezira at length about it yesterday. He said that he had never seen troops at such different levels. Some are outstanding fighters, masters of their weapons. Others seem to be holding a spear in their hands for the first time. What all of them completely lack is coordination as a troop. Each of them is fighting only for themselves, with no support for those around them.

In battle, the best will quickly wear themselves out and become easy targets even for an inferior opponent."

He let his words sink in before continuing.

"If Senezon is hard on them now, they will learn soon enough to organise their forces and coordinate rather than stand as individuals. The weak must be weeded out for those who remain to build trust in each other."

Semiramis nodded. "I realise that, Sargon. But this is not just about the soldiers. If we are to succeed, they need the entire city behind them. Who will cook for them? Who will forge the weapons? Who will fix the walls? We cannot afford to turn the city council against us."

"You are their queen," he replied. "They are who they are because of you."

"And they are my people, whom I listen to as you listen to your šaganas," she said firmly. Then more placatingly, she said, "Give them time, Sargon. The fact that our people are not fighting against each other but beside each other is a completely new experience for them. Mistrust runs deep, still. We must not make the citizens of Nineveh feel like slaves. I am sure that, in time, the soldiers will see progress from their training. Then we won't need to wield the stick anymore."

. He saw the logic in her words. With a sigh, he said, "So be it. Let's see if I can get Senezon to treat his troops gently enough to please Governor Samše."

A smile crept onto his lips at the thought of the hot-headed warrior's reaction, and infected Semiramis, too.

Fifteenth Chapter:
The Hunters

"Wouldn't this be a good time for our troops to take a break, Šagana Senezon?"

"Now?" Senezon asked, furrowing his brow. "They're just getting into shape, and you want to take a break?"

"If they take a break, they can better process what they've learned," the woman insisted.

"There's not much to process" growled the fighter. "Step, push, strike. That's all they need to remember."

"And there was that turn you taught them earlier," the woman spoke eagerly. She sounded like a schoolgirl who had just made an important connection in her mind. "That was completely new for them. Believe me. I've had good experiences with giving soldiers regular breaks. It boosts morale."

Senezon sighed. "I pray to Addad that he will also strengthen his armies morally in the same way when he attacks Nineveh. Then we can safely regroup every two hours while his army stops to process what it's learned." The woman looked wounded by his comment. "All right, all right!" he conceded. "My jokes used to be better, too. Somehow, everything gets soft in this city." In resignation, he signalled the nearest unit to stop what their drills. The men and women sank gratefully to their knees, and the doctors rushed in to minister to their bumps and bruises.

Senezon was grumpy. The night before, when the king had told him about the governor's demand to treat the soldiers better, he'd almost offered to resign.

"Drill *less?*" he'd shouted, his voice echoing through the officers' mess. He slammed his fist on the table. "They're all ten years younger than me, at least. They should be able to handle even more. They're too comfortable and the ladies are too hoity-toity. They find anything that even makes them start to sweat revolting. If the stuck-up geese had their way, they'd spend the whole night at the shooting range and that's all."

Sargon nodded understandingly. "We both know that perseverance and drills are necessary. That's not going to change. You just have to train them more gently."

"More gently!" the broad-shouldered fighter aped his king, but Sargon let it pass. Senezon needed to blow off a little steam first, but he would do as ordered. "Should I also sing them a lullaby to make them feel comfortable around me?" he growled, but he was already capitulating.

Because of the type of hand-to-hand combat that Senezon was teaching Nineveh's troops, the heroines got lost in the crowd, robbing them of any opportunity to stand out individually. The reluctance of some of them to fight side by side with common soldiers was clearly written on their faces. The general knew that several female soldiers had already tried to convince the queen that this form of warfare was beneath them. Semiramis had then explained to them that the purpose of war was not to preserve the soldiers' dignity of the, but to preserve the lives of Nineveh's citizens. If they were too good for that, they would have no career as an officer. That had had the desired effect.

Finally, Senezon found a compromise. Half the time, the spearmen and spearwomen could practise ranged combat, but the other half was devoted to increasing their skills as a close combat unit. They were still only fighting imaginary horsemen, as Gusur did not yet have any cavalry ready for action, but that would change by the end of the week. *I hope they'll finally understand the advantage of working as a unit then*, Senezon thought.

He had quite different problems with the dilapidated state of the barracks in the south of the city. Robbed of its purpose, it had until recently served as no more than a cheap storage area. Even after the buildings had been repaired, merchants had still tried to store their goods on the barracks grounds. One morning before manoeuvres, Senezon had even found a shepherd with his flock there. After that, he ordered the area to be secured with a permanent guard. Slowly, the compound regained its military order. The guard troops did their job with zeal, diligently scrutinising all new arrivals. Senezon could only hope that same zeal was maintained when they were facing opponents far more dangerous than Nineveh's merchants.

All at once, there was movement among the guard at the barracks gate , until one person finally emerged from the group. A woman in a flowing cloak and wearing the insignia of Nineveh's ugula approached Senezon. *Her cloak's far too pristine for her ever to have fought in it,* Senezon noted with disdain.

When she had approached to within a few steps, the woman saluted formally and spoke. "Šagana Senezon. I am Nuw-nim-sum, ugula of the third archers at the south gate. I am here to report about five hundred troops approaching the south gate."

Senezon's was suddenly alert. "What kind of troops?"

"Almost exclusively foot soldiers, General. Heavy infantry. There are a few individual horsemen securing the flanks, and a few wagons are also travelling with them."

Senezon nodded—some good news for a change.

"That sounds to me like our troops arriving from the border. Send out some horsemen to make sure. The soldiers are to be led by the quickest route here to the barracks." The woman bowed and hurried back to carry out her orders. Senezon turned to his adjutant. "Exercises are over for the day. All men and women are to assist in housing the new arrivals. Tell the cooks to get to work immediately. These troops haven't eaten anything decent for days. Then send a messenger to King Sargon. Tell him that Akkad's troops have arrived in Nineveh."

Just then, Prince Gusur was in the hills north of the city with a small group of horsemen. Queen Semiramis had offered him members of her guard, whom he already knew from the ship, as escorts. He was grateful to have their familiar faces around him in the strange hills. His task was proving to be far more difficult than he'd expected. As his father had foreseen, Nineveh did not maintain mounted units. Nor did they use chariots, as they felt safe behind their walls and the terrain in the area was too rocky for chariots, anyway. The city's merchants mostly used mules and donkeys to haul their carts along the roads. Horses were rare and expensive commodity in Nineveh. With some pressure from the queen, Gusur was finally able to buy eight horses—in-

tended for a customer far to the north—from a breeder.
But the scouts needed more than thirty horses and riders
to do their job properly. Gusur had therefore changed
his original plan to train a few of the spearmen and
archers to ride and was now looking for recruits among
a group that already could, and who owned their own
horses: hunters.

Although the population of Nineveh lived mainly
from agriculture and fishing, hunters still roamed in
the forests and foothills of the mountains, where bears,
deer and foxes lived. Their meat, as well as their hides,
fetched high prices in the city. Lions were also numerous and posed a constant threat to the flocks of sheep.
As the heraldic animal of Ishtar, however, the lion stood
under the protection of the goddess—only the queen
could hunt them. Shepherds, however, were allowed to
kill a lion to defend their flock, and every shepherd carried a slingshot, some even a bow. But in close combat,
a lion was invincible. Gusur, familiar with neither a bow
nor a slingshot, always kept a respectful distance when
he saw one of Ishtar's sacred animals.

They had been hiking for about three hours when
Gusur smelled smoke and roasted meat. Soon they saw
a fire ahead, around which a small group was gathered.
Horses were grazing a little away along a river. Slowly,
he and his companions approached the fireplace, but
they were immediately spotted by a guard, who announced their approach with a loud shout. In seconds,
the men and women at the fire had drawn their bows
and positioned themselves in the semi-darkness. Gusur
ordered his companions to stop and slowly moved towards the group, his hands raised.

"Have no fear. We come in peace and would ask you
to allow us to rest at your fire."

A woman approached him. She had lowered her bow but kept the arrow on the string. Her dark eyes observed the new arrivals attentively.

"What are you doing in these woods? Can't find your way back to the city?"

Gusur shook his head. "We're looking for hunters who know how to handle a horse."

"I see. Are you the southman who defeated ten soldiers in Nineveh?"

Gusur smiled. "Stories grow the more they're told. There were only nine and I had two helping me," he said.

The woman seemed satisfied with his answer. "If it's really you, at least you're honest. Not bad for a southman," she said.

"We have our good points too," he agreed. "May we join you?"

"There's not much meat and we're hungry," the woman said.

"Then let us share what we've brought. Nineveh supplies its fighters well."

That was enough. The hunters made room for the strangers by the fire. *Recruitment has begun*, Gusur thought.

"No, the townspeople in Nineveh really know nothing about horses," said the woman, who had introduced herself as Urta. They were sitting around the fire, sharing the meat and bread. Gusur was even able to offer his hosts a wineskin they'd brought, which was happily received by the hunters. The atmosphere relaxed more and more. "My family has been breeding horses for hunting for seven generations. I couldn't live in Nineveh's stinking alleys. The walls smother me. Out here, I have the wind and freedom," Urta said.

"What about bandits? And lions?", Gusur asked.

"It's not half as bad as the townspeople think," she laughed. "They usually go for richer prey that's easier to catch."

"Bandits out here are like the highwaymen on the big trade routes," added one of her companions. "They try to trap you the same way, every time, with traps only a stranger can get caught in."

"And the lions?" Gusur pressed.

"Ishtar's companions can be a problem," the woman admitted. "In the dry season, especially. When the rivers are low, the hungry beasts will even venture near a fire to snatch a horse."

Gusur saw that one of his companions from Nineveh was looking around nervously, but he decided not to worry about lions, not as long as their hosts remained calm by the fire. The group, twelve men and women in total, were perfect for the scouts he'd been tasked with finding. They knew the area and obviously knew how to ride. How could he win them over?

"Tell us something about yourselves," the woman urged him. "This is the first time we've seen men from the realm of Marduk. We've heard that you are great warriors. Tell us about your battles."

"It's true that our fighters are brave," Gusur said, "but we have found no less bravery here in your country. But our life is different. We do not have cities like Nineveh, surrounded by such strong walls. Many of us live in tents and travel with our flocks, following the grass. Even King Sargon prefers the freedom of the desert to the cities. Just like you, we live with horses. But we also have camels, which are better in the desert. I have two horses myself. They're at home, waiting for my return."

"And who's riding them while you're away?" Urta asked.

"My sister, for sure. She's younger. She grew up with them." He felt a pang in his chest at the thought of the family he'd left behind when he had followed his father north. How much time had passed since then? Three weeks? Changing over to the night had disoriented him. It had to be a little more than three weeks, he decided. He continued: "My unit is fully mounted, along with four other units I command. We mostly secure the area around our marching troops and intercept archers before they can reach us. And we're also hunters. There are many antelope and hares on the steppes."

"And your weapons?"

"Mostly spears and hand weapons. We don't have the metal you use for your arrows, and our wood is not as strong as your, so we can't build bows as large as what you carry. So we have to get close to our quarry."

"I want to see you ride," Urta suddenly said, and she stood up without waiting for his answer. "Those were all fine words you used to describe yourself, but we can we see who you really are on horseback—and what you want from us."

Gusur looked at her. "I think you already know who I am and what I want," he replied. "I am looking for good riders as scouts. I want people able to warn Nineveh in time when an attack comes."

"We work for our families, no one else" the woman replied firmly. "There is nothing the townspeople can offer us that we don't already have."

"If Addad conquers Nineveh, he will not limit himself to the city," Gusur said.

"The gods' quarrels are not ours. Addad, Ishtar, Enlil . . . they look down on the temples and buildings and envy each other when one is more revered than another. We honour Anat, our goddess of the hunt, not by crowding into stone houses, but by competing in her light on the backs of our horses, out in the wilds."

"Then let me thank Anat for your hospitality," Gusur said, and he stood and strode to his horse. Urta was clearly pleased to see that he accepted her challenge. They both saddled their horses with woven blankets and fitted their bridles.

"We'll ride on both sides of the stream that leads to the Tigris. Torches mark the halfway point and the end of the course. The first to return to the starting point wins." Gusur had no objections and left the hunters to prepare.

Ugula Sintana, who had accompanied Gusur from the border to Nineveh, came to him with a warning. "Prince Gusur, you will not be able to see much of what lies in your path. If you are hurt in a fall, we may not be able to get you to the city in time to save you."

"I trust my horse to see the way and Marduk to guide me. It is his will that these people become our scouts. We must win them over. Marduk will be with me until the last day."

"I pray to Ishtar that this is not your last night," the woman murmured, with little conviction. But she stepped aside and let Gusur pass.

Excitement had arisen among the hunters, sitting so idly by the fire just a short time before. *A match*, they whispered excitedly to each other and looked for the best places from which to watch the spectacle. Urta seemed relaxed about the race as she guided her horse sedately to the starting point.

Gusur was more nervous than he had let on to his companion. In daylight, he had always won his races.

But here, the torches and the weak moonlight only allowed him to see a few steps ahead. And he had only been riding this horse for three days. Slowly, they had gotten to know each other, but now and then the horse had jerked or flinched in a way that he couldn't quite interpret. It was fast and had enjoyed being given the freedom to set its own pace out in the steppes. How would it handle a race in unfamiliar terrain? Was it madness or recklessness that had driven him to accept Urta's challenge? He needed scouts, and these hunters were made for the role, but they would not follow anyone they did not respect. Victory in a race was a sign they understood.

The start and finish point of the race was marked with four torches. A bare path led west in front of him, following a small stream towards the moon, which glimmered behind the clouds. From the start, Gusur could see the two torches that marked the first stage. A glow further back showed him the point from which they would return. There were no trees or bushes, which was good, but here and there, rocks of different sizes blocked the track.

A hunter approached with a torch: the starting signal. Gusur's mind was on nothing but his horse and the race course. From the corner of his eye, he was just able to see the man swing the torch down signalling the start. His horse was already leaping forward, and his companions, standing at the start, cheered him on, banging their swords against their shields.

Gusur hardly heard it. Every fibre of his body was taut. The muscles of his legs felt his galloping steed's every movement. He was leaning far forward to better spy out the ground ahead, his face almost touching the animal's neck when it moved its head back. The path raced towards them. Gusur suddenly saw a boulder in their path and signalled the horse with a twitch of the reins to go around the obstacle on the right. But he lost important time.

Urta had started just as fast and kept level with the man from Akkad. She knew her horse, and both knew the race course well. Across the stream, she could see the stranger—he was showing himself to be a worthy opponent. *He shies from nothing,* she noted, appreciative. *These rocks are treacherous, and his eyes are not used to the night. He is wise to let his horse guide him.* The man was a better rider than she'd expected, and Urta spurred her horse to stay level. His swing around the boulder gave her a lead of about half a length as they passed the first stage marker.

Gusur's horse raced past the two flaming markers and kept on towards the turning point, flickering still far ahead on a plateau. A rush of emotions had taken over his body, a feeling he knew from the competitions of his homeland. Horse and rider became one. They shared every step and together sensed the path between the rocks, focussed completely on the finish line.

He felt as if he was in a desert storm, felt the wind furrow his face and blow his long hair back. All thought of wars, of gods, of plans had disappeared. There was only him, the horse, and the path they were racing along. The fear he'd felt at the start was gone. The path now lay clearly before him, whether through his own eyes or his horse's. Both wanted to win. They hurtled onward together.

Urta had to devote all her attention to her own horse and race. She spurred her stallion on and turned at the halfway point just ahead of the man from Akkad. Now it was back to the camp, and she would not give up the lead. But the man's horse seemed only now to show its true mettle. It gained steadily and had already overtaken her as they passed the torches of the final stage. Urta cracked her heels into her horse's sides and whispered, "Faster, my love. You are the wind!" And her horse, too, found more speed.

Gusur had merged completely with his horse. He no longer needed to peer into the darkness. They knew the route. Even before they caught sight of the boulder, he had already made his decision. He set himself to jump. The horse understood his rider's signal and carried him in a tremendous leap over the boulder. A shout went through the crowd of spectators, whom they were now approaching rapidly. Gusur was ahead. He raced across the finish line and let his horse trot out slowly before turning back. Ugula Sintana and the others were running towards him cheering.

"Madman!" someone shouted from afar. "Only a madman could beat this champion."

He'd won? Gusur, dismounting, almost slumped to the ground as he realised he'd actually won. His horse was trembling and his own body, every fibre, felt as if pierced by needles. He could barely hold himself up.

The man with the torch, who had given the start signal, stepped up to congratulate him and confirm the result. Urta dismounted and led her horse to him. She stroked his horse's neck and spoke lovingly: "You have a strong master. Guard him well. He is worth it." Turning to the prince from Akkad, she said, "It was a pleasure to see you ride. You are a worthy adversary. Anat gave you the victory. She will watch over you in the future."

"It would be presumptuous of me to expect that from Anat. Your hunters are the best guards I could wish for." He looked at her hopefully.

"We do not guard walls," Urta said firmly. "Our service is to Anat and the hunters."

"There is nothing else I would ask of you," Gusur said. Then he had an idea. "Let us arrange a race once a week, in Anat's honour. We will build a track outside the city. Between races, the riders can hunt and train, each in their own separate area around the city. Anyone who disturbs a rider in their training is an enemy of Anat and Ishtar and shall be punished accordingly."

The woman nodded. "You are fast, Gusur, and you think on your feet. But there is wine to be finishes at the fire. And there is much to discuss."

Sixteenth Chapter:
Everyday Life in Nineveh

"The next petitioner is the merchant Wuti-nan, son of Shi-kul," announced the guard at the door to the council chamber. The scribe took new clay tablets and pressed their surfaces smooth to record the new process. Semiramis sat on her throne in front of the statue of Ishtar, Samše sat to her right and the high priestess to her left. Sargon sat a little apart with several female officers. Unless military questions arose, he had no active part here.

A large city like Nineveh required that justice be done, and decisions made daily to order the lives of its inhabitants—it was said that there were more than fifty thousand. Sargon had usually tried to avoid such council meetings in his capital, Akkad. He preferred the open countryside to the city's narrow streets. Town structures in the realm of Marduk were also not as fixed as Nineveh's. The frequent floods along the lower course of the rivers prevented such large cities from being permanently established. Settlements grew towards each other until their borders merged.

But in Nineveh, the divisions of the city were planned. Entire districts were modified or rebuilt, again and again. The city's administrative apparatus occupied a significant space in the life of Nineveh—spatially, too, as Sargon had noticed when visiting the archives. Such order had a number of advantages, he had to admit. With the help of the written records, ownership could be traced back through many generations.

Traders also appreciated the stability and predictability that Ishtar's realm offered. In the markets of Nineveh, weapons made of gleaming metal, fabrics representing the highest arts of weaving, valuable cedar wood, fine pottery, but also slaves and animals were offered in large quantities. The profits seemed extraordinary, and the leasing income for the market stalls was an essential source of income for the city.

This was also why the merchant had been granted an audience with the city council to present his case. He arrived wearing a dark woven tunic with a braided belt that held a leather pouch. His hair was combed back in long curls in the manner of kings. His beard was perfectly trimmed, and he wore rings and bracelets that suggested impressive wealth. He crossed the room confidently with long strides and knelt before his queen and the image of the goddess.

"Hail, goddess. Hail to you, great queen," he began his speech. "I thank you for granting me some of your time."

"We salute you Wuti-nan, son of Shi-kul," Semiramis replied. "We are happy to hear the concerns of the friends of our city."

The businessman bowed to Samše and the council elders before turning back to the queen with his request. He ignored the king from Akkad.

"Your Majesty, my wish concerns a caravan of two thousand four hundred minae of copper and three hundred and sixty minae of tin destined for the city's weaponry. We were able to acquire the metals from distant Cyprus for your troops. My family has spared no expense or effort to provide Nineveh with the very best to defend the city."

This sounds like the prelude to a price negotiation, Semiramis thought, but she said nothing and let him continue talking.

"After the long march through the desert, the caravan has reached the Tigris at Tarbisu. It is now travelling downstream by ship and will reach Nineveh next week. To unload the copper and tin, however, we need a stronger dock than the one at the west gate. Without that, the ships will have to travel to Nimrud, where there is a fortified jetty, and then make their way back overland from there. This will delay the arrival by more than a week, and I am concerned about the safety of the precious metals."

You're concerned about the costs more, you old rascal, thought Sargon. *What is this ridiculous request to the queen? The courtiers can take care of things like this.*

Before Semiramis could answer, Samše indicated that she wanted to add something. Semiramis let her speak. "Your Majesty, Wuti-nan and his clan have been preferred suppliers to Nineveh for generations. The city owes much to their skill. The council has resolved to increase our trade with the peoples to the north and west. To the north of the city, the river does not have the same torrential force it has further south. We had therefore planned to expand the docks and make Nineveh a transfer point for traders."

Sargon remembered how, on their way from the border, it was only from Nimrud that they could navigate the river in large ships. Along the way, they had seen many barges bringing trade goods from the north to the city to sell or reload onto caravans.

Samše continued, "We have already laid the foundations for a landing stage at the south gate, one that can also carry heavy metals and other goods. The wood for the superstructure is ready and we could complete it quite quickly."

"It sounds to me as if everything is already prepared for the arrival of the goods, Samše. What is preventing the dock from being completed?" the queen asked. Sargon guessed the answer.

"It is the same dock I referred to earlier, the one our troops were working on, Your Majesty. We lack workers, and the work on the dykes and in the fields cannot be postponed. However, if we could deploy fifteen units of the city guard, the new dock would be completed before the ships arrive in Nineveh."

Sargon drew a sharp breath. Fifteen units meant taking half of their battle-ready troops. That would be serious setback, especially now that so many of the soldiers were just beginning to understand tactics and develop routines. He felt everyone's eyes on him as Semiramis asked, "What does King Sargon think about the plan?"

The Akkadian had a clear answer on the tip of his tongue. Still, he did his best to retain his outward composure.

"The representative of Ishtar has asked me to prepare her city for Addad's attack. We know that attack could come at any time. Addad's fortress is in the mountains north of the city, and he will strike from there. If we're attacked while our soldiers are working in the south, they won't reach the northern walls in time." When the queen remained silent, he went on. "Our soldiers have been practising manoeuvres together, non-stop, every night. They are starting to bond as a troop. A construction project like this will tear them apart again. We must not stop."

Semiramis had expected this response. She shared his concerns. At the same time, the shipment of copper and tin was vital. The troops needed more swords to reach full strength. And she could not entirely ignore the trade that made this city as great as it was. *Ishtar, Goddess!*, she thought. *How much time do we have? Do we dare to interrupt the exercises?*

She had made her decision, a compromise to satisfy both sides as much as possible. She spoke first to the trader. "Wuti-nan, son of Shi-kul, we thank you and your clan for your efforts on behalf of our city. Travel in the knowledge that your caravan will be able to unload at a dock in Nineveh that can handle your precious cargo."

To Sargon she said, "The caravan is carrying important metals. We will need them to equip our troops properly. If the cargo arrives on time, it will also help our defences. Deploy fifteen units to help build the dock for nine nights."

Samše was ready to dismiss the merchant, but the queen wasn't finished. "I also agree with the commander that we must not interrupt our joint exercises. Every third night, I expect the troops—all of them—to be at the training grounds. In nine days, I expect the dock to be finished, after which the soldiers are to return to their barracks."

That was the end of the matter.

Shortly before the council meeting, Samše had called the merchant to her to coordinate his request to Queen Semiramis. She had cleverly arranged to present the influential businessman's request directly to the queen and not to the council, and she had watched with satisfaction as Semiramis had struggled to decide. Construction on the jetty to the south had been idle for far too long and Nineveh was falling further out of favour with the merchants with every day wasted on exercises for an attack that would never happen. The cargo of copper and tin offered her a perfect oppor- tunity to once again assert her control over the fate of the city. Just before the meeting, Samše had also met with the soldiers she had charged with intercepting the messenger. They had been gone longer than expected. Their leader explained that they wanted to make sure before they returned that the prisoner was indeed being held out of sight—one more superfluous project avert- ed. Now all she had to do was put an end the exercises that were tying so many workers. After so many defeats, it had been a good day.

"Every third day?"

Senezon was beside himself when Sargon told him about the queen's decision. He hurled his beer mug into a corner where it shattered, the brown liquid splash- ing out and running down the walls. "Has she lost her mind? What did that slimy money-bag offer her to make her skirt the council? Let them find other craftsmen!"

Sargon let him rage. His general usually calmed down on his own once he had let off steam.

"Yesterday I finally had them to the point where they stayed in formation for two exercises without step- ping out of line," Senezon continued. "The women are the worst, the ones who always have to stand out. Their governor's just the same. Why can't she just mind her business and let us men do our duty? No sooner do we get things in order than she comes and interferes and undermine all our good work. No wonder no man

wants to get involved with the hag." According to ru-
mour, the governor lived alone with her cats in a palace
near the temple. She was said to have had relationships
with younger craftsmen but was not known to have a
steady partner.

Even after many weeks with Semiramis, Sargon
found it difficult to comprehend the structures of a so-
ciety dominated by women. In Akkad, a powerful, single man in middle age would not be able to turn down
offers from future fathers-in-law. He would take a wife,
if only to ensure the continuity of his clan through children. With women, fertility dried up earlier. *Could Samše
still have children?* he asked himself. If not, why did she
need a husband at all? It struck him that Semiramis
had also never spoken of a husband or children. He
himself had already acknowledged four children as his,
three boys and a girl. Their mothers ran his household.
But here?

Senezon had no idea that his king's thoughts were
wandering far from the training of the troops. He was
beginning to calm down and was poking at the sand
with a stick, sorting out his thoughts.

"The governor wants fifteen units for the construction. Most of them will be swordsmen, our strongest.
She can't do anything with the scrawny archers, and
she won't get our Akkadians for that. So she'll need
three units of spearmen as well if she doesn't want to
disband the city guard."

"I can't imagine that," Sargon said, returning to
more pressing questions. "The guard is needed at the
market. And at the gates, too, to collect tolls. She won't
want to do without the money."

"Money, money, money!" sneered Senezon. "Is it always about one thing in this damned city? You can't

take a step here without someone holding out their hand. Marduk, I miss the desert and the empty plains!"

Sargon had to agree with him. All the peddlers and their greed were abhorrent to both of them. He sighed. "We have to live with it. We have to accept that we only have the soldiers every three days. It's only three interruptions. In nine days we can continue as before."

"If Addad doesn't attack by then," Senezon said.

"Somehow, I think he's still gathering troops, too," the king said. "Nineveh is a city with mighty walls, even with fewer soldiers. Woranola and her machines can do a lot to stop an attacking army."

He stood up.

"Use the time to explore the city. Take Gusur with you when he's not riding out. I want you to know the main roads and routes to the barracks so well that you can lead troops by the quickest route to any point on the walls."

Senezon grumbled. "First I become a nursemaid for wimps who think they're soldiers, and then you make me a city guide. I wonder what Marduk has in store for me next." But he didn't put up any more of a fight. Sargon left him and went to seek out Semiramis in the palace.

The queen was sitting on a terrace on the roof of the palace, high above the city. Her seat was a simple pedestal padded with blankets. Beside her lay countless clay tablets, which she examined, altered as she saw fit, and confirmed with her seal. A small oil lamp illuminated her workplace. She wore a long, layered dress held at the waist by the woven belt her mother had given her. Ishtar was often depicted in such a dress. Semiramis felt the confidence in her body when she wore the dress to honour the goddess and the belt in memory of her mother. *Can they see me now?*, she wondered, looking up at the cloudy sky. *Did I make the right decision?* she asked silently into the darkness. No answer came. She returned her attention to the clay tablets and the work that had to be completed.

She heard Sargon coming. She recognised him immediately by the length of his stride. *None of the courtiers can keep up with him,* she thought, amused. She was still impressed at how he had held himself together earlier when she had taken the soldiers from him. *Ah Sargon,* she thought. *How ironic that in my own city I can rely most on the leader of the people with whom we are at war. Were at war,* she corrected herself. *Those days are over, though my city council may think otherwise. Addad has brought our destinies together, and from him comes the real danger we face. But what happens when that danger is overcome, or if it does not arise at all?* Loneliness and responsibility weighed heavily on the queen, and this time the familiar darkness offered no comfort.

"Senezon has his orders," Sargon said when he came to her. "He's going to reorganise the training and will use the remaining time to familiarise himself with Nineveh's roads."

"Did much get broken in the process?" she asked, turning to him, and he saw the slight smile on her lips.

"Nothing that can't be replaced," he replied. He sat down next to her, and his gaze wandered over the city and up to the sky, where the clouds were piling up. They had not looked out at the night together since their time together on the river.

"Senezon is proud of his work and what he's achieved with your troops," he said. "He's worried that they'll forget everything if Addad attacks us unprepared."

"They are *our* troops, Sargon," she reminded him. Her smile had disappeared. "That hasn't changed today."

"You could have asked for time to think about it, to coordinate with me in private," he said. She heard his disappointment clearly. "Now Samše has the troops back under her control."

"She serves the city, and the city serves me," Semiramis stated. He did not understand the symbolism, but it was important. So, patiently, she tried to explain her behaviour to him. "As representative of the goddess, I must make decisions about the city before Samše's eyes. Hesitation would have been read as weakness. Trade is vital for the city. Besides, we need the metals for weapons."

She placed a hand on his sword arm, which rested on his knee.

"Sargon, we both know the risk. If this becomes our moment of weakness, Addad will attack Nineveh within the next nine days. Our mutual trust must not weaken." There it was again, that haunting look deep in her eyes. Sargon felt her hand on his. He knew she was right. Delay would weaken their defence against Addad, true. But discord between them would destroy it utterly. The Akkadian sighed.

"And when the nine days are over? Can we go back to regular training, or is your governor planning another garden or tower or something?"

The smile had returned to her face. "Nineveh is over a thousand years old. Structures like that can wait." She felt a warmth in her loins as he returned her smile, and she felt his approval. Ishtar was close.

"The whole town is one big huckster's market," Senezon observed as they made their way through the alleys. Gusur could not disagree as he dodged around a porter who was placing earthenware jars on a rack to attract a shopper's eye. They had initially chosen the north barracks as their starting point for exploring the city's streets, hoping to orient themselves better—the city walls in the north and east were closer there. But after just two blocks, their sense of direction faded in the hustle and bustle of traders, slaves, porters, herds of animals, and crowds pushing steadily through the big city.

Two scribes were walking with Senezon and Gusur, both to give them information and to take careful note of their every instruction. Senezon frowned. *Does it never stop?* he wondered, when a scribe produced yet another new tablet to make notes. *You can't fart here without them scratching it down?* He never knew what the marking on their tablets meant. But Semiramis had once read him a summary of his drills, and Senezon had been shocked at how meticulously everything, even unimportant comments, had been recorded. He had even heard that there were storerooms in the palace where the clay tablets were organised and kept. For nothing in the world would Senezon want to exchange his fate with that of a slave who spent the day stacking and arranging clay tablets.

Meanwhile, Gusur's attention was drawn to a stall that sold hides. They were similar to the skins he had seen with the hunters. The vendor was instantly at his side. "Wonderful, aren't they? The best skins in Nineveh, I swear it. Just look at this texture! Run your fingers over the surface just once. It will fit like a second skin.

It's just the thing to get the respect you deserve as a šagana."

"You'll get nothing from me if you start wearing rags like that," Senezon growled. "We have to move on." The shopkeeper saw a potential sale disappearing and he stopped Gusur, who was about to turn away. "You're the leader of the riders, aren't you? I would be honoured if you wore one of my skins. I can let you have it for only two minae of copper."

Gusur made an effort to turn the man down politely. "Thank you, but no."

"One mina and thirty shekels," the seller persisted. Gusur shook his head and followed Senezon, who was already a few steps away. "One mina and ten!" the man shouted desperately and hurried after him, holding the hide in front of him. Gusur said nothing. "One mina. It's what I paid for it myself." That was too much for Senezon. He drew his dagger and held the point to the man's throat. "One more word and your stand will have a new hide to sell: your own!" he snarled.

The man turned pale and stammered, "But, but . . ."

"No buts. Take your rag and get back to your shed before I really get upset." The salesman had a retort on his lips but decided to keep it to himself when he saw Senezon's expression. He retreated.

"Nineveh is one big huckster's shop," the fighter sighed. "Or did I say that already?"

"Three times since we left the barracks," Gusur laughed. He was in a good mood and his thoughts were still on the horse race of the day before. He was proud of his riders, who had treated the townspeople to an impressive race. King Sargon had shaken each one's hand and congratulated them on a job well done. Now the whole town was talking about nothing but the horse race, and the prince was being admired like a hero. But that did not improve his friend's mood.

The alley they were now following crossed a road that had a dark, solid surface. It was also wider, with enough space between the stalls on each side for two carts to pass without getting in each other's way. City officials had explained to them that Nineveh had three different types of street. There were the wide boulevards, like the one leading from the Šibaniba Gate to the temple, that were paved with kiln-fired bricks. Along these streets, the merchants were only allowed to set up their stalls on the verges. The second type was paved with dark stone layers that did not soften even when it rained, like the street at which they had now arrived. The rest were covered with clay and were only passable for heavy carts in the dry season.

Senezon beckoned one of the scribes to him. "If we need to get the soldiers to the wall quickly, we must be able to reach a road as soon as possible. Which road runs closest to the barracks?" he asked.

The scribe, from Nineveh, thought for a moment. "That would be the road that goes past the Weavers Well. It's very long. To the north it goes as far as the processional road and to the south as far as the bridge over the Khosr."

The Akkadian nodded. "Sounds good. That can be our way to the north wall. What's the quickest way out of the city from the boulevard?" he asked.

"Roads branch off the boulevard to all the gates of the north wall. They are all surfaced like this one," the man replied.

"And to the eastern wall? What leads there?" Senezon said.

"The boulevard crosses the city in the north. It leads to the Šibaniba Gate."

Senezon was satisfied. "That's good. Then all we need is a way to get to the Mushalu Gate, the first one on the eastern wall north of the Khosr," the general said. "Can you actually draw on those clay tablets? It would be good to have a map of all that. We could use it to explain our routes to the platoon leaders." The scribe was a little uncertain and consulted with his partner, but they finally agreed to produce clay tablets for Senezon that showed the roads he wanted.

"Then get to work on it now," Senezon ordered. "You'll be doing something far more useful than writing down all the nonsense I spout."

The scribes had done a good job. The next day, Senezon and Ezira were able to present their king with a plan for the movement of the troops from the northern barracks. They stood with the other officers involved in planning in Sargon's quarters. Each had a map of the city in front of them and could estimate the distances the troops would have to cover in an emergency.

Sargon had reservations. "Our ground troops can easily reach the gates via the boulevard, certainly. But we will need to get the archers and spearmen from the southern barracks up on the walls more urgently. They'll have to cross the entire city."

Woranola, attending the officers' meeting for the first time, tried to allay the king's concerns.

"Sir, we grew up in this city. My soldiers know every alley. The road that Senezon's troops take from the Weavers Well goes south of the Khosr to Ashur Gate. There is a direct road from the south barracks which crosses it, so we won't have to squeeze through narrow alleys like Senezon and his troops. Our soldiers also wear much lighter armour than yours. We will be on the walls faster than you think."

Sargon looked at the young woman. At Hofileshgu's suggestion, he had put Woranola in charge of the archers. Together with the defensive machines, they were crucial in keeping the enemy away from the walls. Unlike Hofileshgu, however, she did not seem to have been in the military for long. She made up for her lack of experience with confidence and perseverance. She wore her hair framed with a narrow band, often coloured or even embroidered—the latest fashion in Nineveh. Her fingers were long and adorned with the kind of marks that Gusur had admired on other women in the city. The recent promotion had increased her self-confidence—she radiated an aura of invincibility. But Sargon was not entirely convinced.

"I appreciate your confidence, Woranola, but I fear you underestimate the distance and obstacles along the way."

"Then let me prove it to you, Majesty," the young woman replied. "We are faster than you think, I am sure."

"So . . . another competition?" Sargon asked with a grin. After the hunters' horse race, all of the higher officers were eager to show off. "A race through the city?" he asked those around him.

Senezon, who also wished that something would finally happen, spoke up. "That's what I want to see, how you fillies are going to cover the distance," he goaded. "By the time you reach the wall you'll be too exhausted to make it up the steps."

"We'll set you up with a few extra jugs of ale in advance, so you can drink yourself a little courage before the battle," the challenger replied spiritedly, but she smiled as she spoke.

Sargon ended the argument. "Then it's decided. You'll have your competition the day after tomorrow. We'll run an exercise to test the routes from the barracks to the walls. Each division will send one unit, fully equipped and in full armour, for the purpose. Your target will be one of the gates in the north, but you will only find out which one when a signal fire is lit on both towers. You can see the towers of all the gates from your barracks. The last unit to reach the wall next to the gate will be on latrine duty next week."

Senezon tightened the strap of his helmet. He didn't want it to get caught on anything in the upcoming run through the city's alleys. As he had done several times already, he called up to the guard on the roof of the barracks: "Well?"

"Nothing, sir," the man replied. Senezon could not see the guard, but he knew he had not turned his gaze from the city. It had been dark for two hours and the usual noise of business sounded from the streets. The king had ordered that the exercise not be announced, to practise the advance under realistic conditions. Senezon was well aware that if they were actually attacked and panic gripped the people, then getting through would probably be even more difficult. *As if we don't have enough obstacles already,* he thought grimly.

He had selected his unit carefully, assembling it evenly with men from Akkad and soldiers from Nineveh. Local knowledge could not hurt if they had to improvise and take detours. The soldiers knew what they would face if they failed and arrived at the gate too late.

He could rely on them. Then a call rang out: "Sir! The signal. It's from the Mushalu Gate!"

Senezon recalled the map of the city and asked one of the soldiers from Nineveh, "That's the gate north of the Khosr, isn't it?"

"Yes, sir. There's a road to it off the boulevard that's not very busy. We should be able to advance quickly."

"But we're going a different way," the Akkadian replied, shaking his head. "The gate's exactly at our level. Can you lead us through the alleys?"

The man hesitated. "Sir, there are many gardens in that district, and the shearers workshops, too. People avoid the area because the roads are better paved elsewhere."

"Then we'll have fewer traders in our way. Through the alleys!" ordered Senezon. The race had begun.

Woranola had seen the starting signal at the same time. "Our destination is Mushalu Gate," she said to her unit. Nineveh's men and women nodded. "Stay close on the north road! Then the wagons will see us sooner and can move aside. Save your strength at the start! On the boulevard you can move faster, but it's only five hundred metres until we turn into Mushalu Street. We will only be able to move slowly through there. Let's go!" With her last words she was already leading the way into the alleys of Nineveh. Her soldiers followed in close formation.

Senezon's run ground to a halt just a few steps outside the barracks when a group of slaves crossed their path. The men and women were chained together at the ankles, and the unit had to let them pass before they could continue. Then they passed through the stalls of the fur and cloth merchants, who swore furiously at them if they knocked over a basket in passing or if one of the men tripped over a guy rope and it came loose. *All one big hawker's shop,* Senezon thought angrily. The hustle and bustle at the stalls seemed particularly bad today. The Ninevehans in his unit were now shouting constantly, warning people to move aside as the unit came through. This had some effect, but not always. Senezon's reservoir of curses was put to ample use that day.

Next they came to an area where the ground was spongy and soggy. A sewer had overflowed, and the filthy broth of sewage mixed with the rubbish and sand in the alley. *A sign of impending latrine duty?* the superstitious šagana wondered in dismay. His shoes dug deep into the mud, and he felt his heavy armour weighing like lead on his shoulders. The men behind him were breathing hard, but they stayed together. Senezon barely noticed as, dripping with stinking mud, they clanked across a merchant's display of reed mats. The merchant, however, barely held back his anger at the sight of the heavy armaments and the determined faces of the soldiers.

Their route went on between screaming market women, dogs, and goats, and past nobly dressed merchants on their donkey-drawn carts, who took no notice at all of the tumult.

Much later than usual, they finally reached the Weavers Well road, which they recognised immediately from its dark surface. The road led seductively straight and with little traffic to the north. Senezon pulled over the soldier who'd been showing him the way.

"Which alley now?" he shouted.

"Sir, we should really stay on the street," he said, trying to change his šagana's mind once more. These alleys are little used. People only use them if they have a destination here."

"That's what we have," Senezon retorted defiantly, wanting to escape the cursing traders once and for all. "You run ahead!" The man obeyed and they disappeared into the labyrinth of alleys and paths.

Ezira with his spearmen followed a similar plan to Woranola. His barracks were located conveniently to the target, directly on a paved road. He chose a speed that each of them could maintain with full armour, and he kept his group in close formation in the middle of the road. His unit's starting point was between those of the other two, so as long as they did not let the archers overtake them, his soldiers could be sure of avoiding latrine duty. Ezira was not out to achieve the greatest speed. It was more important to him to find out how long it would take fully equipped soldiers to be at the walls ready to fight, and he had accordingly selected members from several units, not just his best runners.

Woranola's unit advanced confidently. They had reached the road north faster than expected and moved at double time, keeping in step. The rhythmic beat of their footfall caught the attention of others using the road, who immediately made way as the group approached. Children chased them, laughing, and traders shouted words of encouragement when the archers passed by.

Woranola was enjoying the run. This was her town, and she knew every house. But at the same time, she knew that she had to beat two more units if she wanted to win. And she had vowed to do so, if only to show up the overbearing Senezon. *Patience*, she told herself. On the boulevard, they were going to overtake both competitors. Until then, she paid attention to her regular breathing and delighted in the shouts of the children and traders.

Senezon's unit was now completely stuck. The alleys were winding, and the high walls made it difficult to find their way. Several times, the soldier from Nineveh had to change direction when the alley turned a different way than he'd expected. Now they had reached a point where the alley ended in front of a house that he was convinced had never stood there before. Senezon was beside himself. He was soaked with sweat, his legs were dripping with mud, and mosquitoes plagued him whenever he came to a stop.

"What now?" he ordered the soldier, who was standing helplessly in front of the house that closed off the alley.

"The road ends here," the man said.

"I can see that," the general replied angrily. "I want to know where we go from here."

"This way was the shortest route through the district. We have to go back and see how we can get around this house." The man started to head back.

"Hold on!" Senezon commanded "You said this path that led through the district, right?" The man nodded.

"Then it also has to continue on the other side of the house. Let's go!" Without waiting for an answer, he stepped inside the building. The anteroom was dark, a single torch the only light. A woman screamed and dropped a jug. It shattered and water splashed across the floor. More cries rang from the background. Senezon ignored the noise and charged on towards the path he knew had to continue behind the house. His soldiers followed. They marched through a courtyard, where several looms were standing, and on into the next room. From there a door led back outside and they found themselves in a garden, its beds watered by channels. A low wall bordered the garden. Behind it, Senezon could see the street squeezing between the rows of houses. Senezon strode on resolutely, through vegetable patches and between bushes. The wall was only waist high, no real obstacle. He jumped over it and his soldiers followed, leaving behind a house in turmoil. Stones were hurled after them but did no damage. Senezon vowed mentally to have a serious word with the city council about building permits in Nineveh.

Woranola's unit, in the meantime, had reached the boulevard. With a battle cry, she urged her women and men on, and they charged along the broad street. When she saw Ezira's slowly advancing unit of spearmen in front of her, her heart rejoiced, and she increased her speed.

A man shouted and Ezira turned his head. Behind them he saw Woranola with her archers rushing along the road at speed, and he increased his pace in turn. It was not far to the turnoff. In the bigger crowd it would be more difficult for Woranola to overtake his unit.

The leader of the archers had no intention of waiting until then. She ran faster and faster along the cobbled street. She was already level with the spearmen. Ezira recognised her plan and kept his unit on the southern side of the road, where the road to the gate would soon turn off. Woranola was forced across to the other side of the road, but she accepted the disadvantage.

Even on the grand boulevard, the race did not go unnoticed. Traders saw them coming from far away and steered their carts to the side to let the competitors pass. As the turn-off approached, the units were level. Ezira slowed down a little to pass between the stones bordering the road, which the lighter archers simply jumped over. Now Woranola's unit was in the lead. With a shout, Woranola urged her archers along the road. *Not far now to the Mushalu Gate*, she thought. *But where is Senezon?*

The šagana drove his weary ground troops on. He had long since stopped counting how many times they'd gotten stuck, either in the mud of the alleys or in a flock of sheep. And he had long since stopped paying attention to the curses and shouts of the farmers when they crossed fields because, yet again, their path was blocked. Now, at least, they could see the Mushalu Gate ahead of them, and with it the prospect of an end to the drudgery. The asphalt road was less than a hundred metres ahead, replacing the never-ending mud like manna from the gods. Senezon gathered up his last reserves, but just before his unit reached the road, Woranola and her archers, at a fast run, passed the point where the alley met the road. Senezon swore aloud.

"Forward!" he urged his comrades-in-arms. "Do you want to clean latrines?" His men and women had also seen the group and once again summoned up their strength. But just as they were turning onto the asphalt, Ezira's spearmen reached them. Angry shouts filled the air out as the soldiers pushed and shoved each other as they ran. Together they rushed towards the gate, which now loomed large before them. The archers were already high on the steps when the other fighters were only beginning their climb. With the last of his strength, Senezon pushed his way up to the tower platform, where his king was already waiting.

Sargon watched the arriving soldiers, while the scribes noted down the order. Woranola's archers were the first to reach the top. They did not seem particularly exhausted from their run. The other two units arrived almost simultaneously a few moments later, but Ezira's spearmen had a slight lead over Senezon's ground troops. The axeman was gasping for breath and looked as if he was about to explode at any moment with anger and disappointment. Sargon congratulated the leader of his bow units.

"The group with the longest route reached their goal first," he noted. "Congratulations on your achievement, Woranola. If we're attacked, it is vital that you are the first on the walls."

"We will not let you down," the young woman promised proudly. With a sideways glance at the exhausted Senezon, she added, "Nor will it be necessary to lead his troops onto the walls. Our arrows and catapults will stop siege machines long before they get that far."

"Famous last words," Senezon muttered irritably. But then he too congratulated her.

Sargon turned to the unfortunate man who'd been his guide. "We'll talk tomorrow about your route through the city. I want to know why it took so long." But he was going to find out much sooner than that.

Seventeenth Chapter:
The Feast

"The man devastated seven fields!" Samše yelled angrily. "And he and his soldiers knocked down four merchants' stalls and destroyed pots and pitchers worth at least three minae of silver. And then there's the damage they did to the silver merchant Wereken's house. His pregnant wife is still in shock and may yet suffer a miscarriage from what she's been through. What is the point of all this?" Her eyes glittered angrily at Sargon, who was appearing before the council and Semiramis to report on the exercise.

"To properly organise our defences, we have to know the shortest routes and we have to learn how quickly we can get our troops to the site of an attack," the king replied. "Practice like this is necessary to keep the city safe from harm."

"Your so-called 'practice' today has done more harm to Nineveh than all the attacks of the last five years put together!" the governor shouted. "Go and practise in the desert! At least you won't hurt anything out there. This is a city. Your soldiers can't just do whatever they want here."

"Until today, we have conducted all of our combat drills on the drill fields that the city council has allocated to us," Sargon insisted. "Today's contest was the first with troops in the city."

"And it had better be the last! I demand an immediate ban on all military exercises inside the city," said the governor. Several councillors nodded their agreement.

Semiramis sat on the throne before the image of the goddess and watched the dispute in silence. *Another point for Samše*, she thought, disappointed. *Why didn't Sargon consult me first? I would have talked him out of the idea. Is he resentful because I ordered the soldiers away to build the jetty?*

The Akkadians had been living in Nineveh for almost two weeks, but they had not yet gotten used to the finely woven order that a large city demanded to stop it descending into chaos. The queen watched closely as governor Samše repeatedly sought eye contact with the councillors as she voiced her accusations, and she seemed to find support among them. *How many are on my side?* Semiramis wondered. The fear of Addad's threat dwindled with each passing day without an actual attack. Would they end up fighting each other again? *Then the god of storms can sit back and see who emerges weakened as the victor—just as he's been doing for so long with my goddess and Marduk.* Semiramis suspected that Addad's attack might still be a long way off. Until then, peace had to prevail in the city. *Sargon is going to be disappointed again*, she thought as she made her decision. She rose to her feet. The room fell silent instantly and all eyes turned to her.

"Today's contest has shown that our soldiers should take the main roads to get to where they are needed. I expect all gal-ugs and platoon leaders to know these roads and ensure that their soldiers do not deviate from them." She needed agreement on this first and paused for a moment to make sure it came. "I do not believe it is necessary at this time to simulate another attack. The gal-ugs have gained enough experience with the routes through the city. From now on, the troops will again focus on their exercises at the barracks."

But this was not enough for Samše. "Your Majesty, we don't need more exercises. They do more harm than good. Let the city return to trade. We live in peace."

Semiramis summoned up all her powers of persuasion and said, "What you call peace is the calm before the storm." She turned to the city council. "It is tempting to think that this calm will last. Many seem to be hoping that the threat was merely imagined, or some sort of misunderstanding. After all, Nineveh has enjoyed many years of peace. 'Why should Addad break that?' you may ask. You have seen the answer for yourselves: because we humans weaken ourselves with our quarrelling and fighting. We say we want the best and to get that we have to push aside whoever is blocking the path we think is the right one to follow. And all along, Addad is laughing at us. He will wait to strike until we are back at each other's throats. Then Nineveh will have nothing left to oppose him."

Turning to Sargon, she said, "Please keep an eye on your officers and soldiers when they pass through Nineveh. Old enmities have been rekindled today, things we wanted to put behind us. Encourage your šaganas to get to know the city and its people better. If your soldiers do not have the trust of Nineveh's citizens, they will never make it through the city in time."

Sargon was irritated at how little the city council seemed to understand. Semiramis saw that he was about to say something and shook her head slightly. The king took a deep breath and kept his retort to himself.

Samše was satisfied with the outcome. In a honey-sweet voice, she changed the subject. "Your Majesty, in three days we will have the next full moon. I plan to throw a banquet in honour of our goddess and would be honoured to welcome everyone present as guests in my humble chambers." Turning to Sargon with an ingratiating smile, she added, "Our queen is wise to advise that your followers study the customs of our land. I would like to extend my invitation to your valiant šaganas as well, if you allow."

Semiramis accepted the offer on behalf of the Akkadians before the king could speak. "That is very generous, Samše. I look forward to having Marduk's ambassador and his šaganas celebrate the full moon with us."

Sargon, realising that the subject was now closed, replied simply, "Governor, we thank you for your generous offer and accept the invitation. May the feast bring our people closer together."

"Is my cloak sitting properly?", Gusur asked his brother-in-arms.

Senezon grunted. "If by that you mean is it on the right person, you can rest easy." He was not happy. He had had to sit for hours while the master barber tamed his long, wavy hair with thin leather cords and then massaged his beard with oil in the Ninevehan fashion. His beard now hung in a perfectly formed rippling washboard shape down to his chest. The king had instructed them to prepare for the banquet at the governor's house, and they had bought cloth for new clothes at the markets, which had then been sewn by Nineveh's tailors. Sargon had also insisted that they have their hair braided and their beards done according to the customs of Nineveh.

Sargon himself wore a dark cloak held together by a heavy chain over a toga. A small dagger in a sheath set with precious stones protruded from his belt. The cloak reached to his ankles, only revealing his sandal-clad feet at the ground. He looked his officers over carefully and, satisfied with their appearance, nodded: time to leave.

Gusur stayed at his father's side as they strode through the streets to the governor's house. The fabric of his garments was finer than anything he had worn before. He felt almost naked as it wafted lightly around his legs as they walked. Senezon, walking beside Ezira and behind the king, missed his weighty battle axe, and the cords in his hair were putting pressure on his scalp— he felt as if he were getting a headache already. After a lot of deliberations, he'd agreed to put on a cloak of flax for the feast. Sheep's wool was repugnant to him after the race through the wool merchants' district. The flaxen fabric was plain but woven in a fine pattern that reflected the light in ever-changing forms as he moved. Unlike his companions, Senezon also wore boots, but he had had new ones made for the occasion. He was peeved at having spent so much on all the frippery. *We look like puffed up peacocks,* he thought. *Real men shouldn't be wasting their time on this.* But his king had asked for it, and he had to comply. *But only for tonight,* he promised himself, as they approached the governor's torchlit house.

Sargon had often passed by this building, which was close to the temple district. Unassuming from outside, it gleamed in colourful splendour on the inside. The guards at the door ushered them in without delay, one hurrying ahead to the governor to announce the guests' arrival. Sargon and his retinue were well known to them.

The entrance hall was brightly lit. Colourful clay rods inserted into the walls formed a mosaic of regular white-and-red patterns, while statues of deities seemed to inspect the arrivals from the many wall niches. Their footsteps echoed on the flagstone-covered floor, while music from the rooms ahead heralded the celebration.

Samše, as the mistress of the house, came out to greet her guests. She wore a blue robe decorated with lace. Her pale skin visible in the deep-cut neckline almost glowed above her breasts. Three long strings of pearls adorned her neck, along with a close-fitting necklace studded with golden plates. On her head, she wore a headband woven with coloured ribbons, while golden leaves covered her forehead like the leaves of trees cover the autumn ground. Glittering earrings dangled like fruit beside her narrow face, her flawless skin making her look almost like a young girl. She bowed so low before her guests from Akkad that Gusur could clearly glimpse her small, shapely breasts beneath her loose-fitting robe.

"Welcome, gentlemen," she said solemnly. "Your presence brings radiance and honour to my humble rooms."

Not that there's any lack of radiance already, Sargon thought. Aloud, however, he said, "Governor Samše, I thank you for the invitation and for your hospitality, also on behalf of my faithful. We are privileged to be part of your celebration."

"Please grant me the pleasure of escorting you personally to the banquet hall, King Sargon," she said. "Hofileshgu and Woranola already await your companions in the garden, which I have had prepared for our brave officers. My courtier will lead them." She gestured towards a young man who had entered the antechamber after her and was kneeling before them. Sargon nodded. The governor took his arm and guided the king through to the courtyard. Gusur, Senezon, and Ezira followed them through the courtyard, but the courtier then turned left to the garden, while the king was led by their hostess into the great hall on the other side. Senezon realised that the layout of the house corresponded to that of the house they had charged through in the race. In the garden, they found five couches decorated with cushions arranged around a fountain. Tables held goblets and clay bowls of fruit for the guests, and musicians played lutes and flutes in the background.

The Ninevehan officers looked up from one of the couches. "Senezon!" exclaimed Woranola in amazement. "What happened to you? You look particularly civilised tonight."

The general was not sure whether she meant it as a compliment or was speaking ironically. Recalling his master's order to make an excellent impression, he did his best. "It is but a poor attempt to do justice to your resplendence, my dear Woranola." She accepted his flattery in good humour and invited him to lie on the couch beside her. Ezira found a seat beside Hofileshgu while Gusur made himself comfortable opposite them.

The sight of Woranola attracted the prince almost magically. She wore a long, yellow dress with fringes that lay over her left leg like the wing of a bird. Her right leg remained completely uncovered from her hip down. Her bare feet, only scantily clad in dainty leather sandals, awakened the young man's imagination. The soft music and the chirping of the crickets lent an enchanting note to the evening that quickly made him forget the world around him. He followed the others' conversation without a word, letting his senses luxuriate in his surroundings.

Samše carried her chin high as she strode with Sargon through the gate to the banquet hall. All eyes were on the governor as she introduced her distinguished guest.

"Welcome, Sargon, ruler of Akkad and representative of Marduk on earth. You enrich my humble home with your presence. May Ishtar bless your every dawn and dusk!" She bowed low.

Sargon responded with an amiable nod and said, "Thank you again for the invitation, Samše, governor of the wonderful city of Nineveh. I am honoured to be here. My greetings also to the high priestess and city council. May Ishtar walk with you and watch over you wherever you go." Samše led him to one of the seats of honour at the head of a long table and then introduced him to her guests, although he already knew most of them. The seat between him and the governor was still empty—the queen had not yet arrived.

A little later, however, a servant appeared and announced Semiramis's arrival to Samše. Before the governor could get to her feet, however, Semiramis had already stepped into the hall. All talk ceased, and even the musicians interrupted their playing. The queen's long dress shone like moonlight into the room. Today, too, Semiramis had dispensed with conspicuous jewellery and wore only a small bandeau to hold back her dark brown hair, which tumbled like silk down her back. Her robe enveloped her slender body in many thin layers, one over the other, and its long train followed as the queen entered the hall. Sargon had risen immediately when Semiramis appeared, and now the other guests jumped up to bow before her. Samše was also on her feet, although with some delay. She had planned the queen's appearance differently and was annoyed that her steward had allowed the most important guest to enter the hall without waiting for her, as they had agreed.

With silent steps, as gentle as a breeze wafting along a river bank, the queen seemed to float past the rows of guests until she came to her place of honour at the head of the table. She nodded graciously to her hostess, and then turned radiantly to Sargon, who bowed silently. Her elegance and beauty once again left him speechless.

When Semiramis spoke, she raised her voice, which penetrated keenly into every corner of the room and touched the hearts of all who heard her. "Praise be to you, Goddess Ishtar, who brings us together in peace this day. We thank you for this evening and for the past month, which has brought so many blessings to our city. Behold, we have made new friends of those we once thought of as enemies. Welcome them, too, to your feast." She let her gaze rest on Sargon for a long time, then turned to the governor and continued, "My thanks go to you, Samše, for allowing us to gather today in your house. You serve your goddess well. May she reward you for your service." Addressing the city council, she said, "And my gratitude also to you, ladies and gentlemen, who guide our city so well. May Ishtar continue to guide your decisions in the coming month."

The high priestess, standing beside Samše, called out loudly, "Hail to Ishtar! Hail to our queen! Hail to our hostess! May she live a thousand years!"

"Hail, hail, hail!" the company replied. Semiramis took her seat, the signal for the others to follow suit. The music resumed. The feast began.

In the garden, Senezon's mood improved more and more as the meal progressed. They were served a hearty stew as a starter, just as he liked it, with plenty of goat meat, leeks, and onions. The bread was freshly baked, crusty, and seasoned with fine herbs. His beer was refilled and refilled again by servants before the dregs could collect at the bottom of the tankard. The beer was cool and not too sweet. He took a delicious draught through his long straw. "I have to say this about your governor, she knows something about food."

Woranola, who was sharing the tankard with him, had to laugh. "You were actually going to say she knows something about brewing beer, weren't you?"

He was feeling particularly generous and said, "Beer, too. Definitely. Strange that she doesn't have a husband."

"Are you thinking about proposing?" Hofileshgu suggested, amused. "With your appetite, you two would make a good match."

Senezon raised his hands defensively "I'd live in fear of my life. She'd either lock me up or knock me off just to keep her huckster stalls safe. No, someone like that's more for our Gusur. Now there's one who wants to please the women."

Gusur turned beet red. Woranola looked now at the prince with interest and toyed with the hem of her dress. Something stirred in the prince as the fabric gradually slipped across her pale legs.

"How do you like the women of Nineveh, Prince Gusur?" she asked.

"They are as delicate and fragrant as the flowers," was all he could stammer out.

"On top of which, they know what they want," Ezira added with a smile.

"And we get it too," Hofileshgu added, pulling the tankard she was sharing with the šagana closer. "Unlike you men." Ezira protested as he tried with feigned desperation to pull the tankard back to him, making all of them laugh.

The next course was served. In the banquet hall, soup was served to the guests of honour after the ritual cleansing of the hands. Sargon looked in amazement at the plates, which were made of blue glass with gold patterns on the rim. Blue was clearly a favourite colour of the governor. Semiramis explained the material to him. "Some years ago, our craftsmen found a way to make glass that shimmers like lapis lazuli. Since then, we no longer depend on the supply of the expensive stones."

"They know their trade well," the king had to admit. He dipped his bread casually into the soup.

"We would be happy to deliver it to Akkad, too," said the governor, adding, "If you can pay in silver."

Sargon did not reply, but Semiramis took up the subject, which she knew was also of interest to the city council. "Trade between our countries would be a great benefit for both sides indeed," she said.

"What goods do you have to trade?" one of the councillors sitting on the other side of Sargon wanted to know.

"In our markets you will find excellent leather and precious stones," the king replied. "We also import incense, tin, copper and ivory from distant lands." He did not mention the wool and fabrics of his homeland. They could not compete with the quality available in Subartu.

"Metals and ivory are always in demand in Nineveh," the councillor replied. "I would be happy to discuss this further with you." Sargon agreed, but the arrival of the entertainers interrupted their conversation.

Four women and four men entered the room. The women wore long chains and bells on their hands and feet that rang with every step. The men had brought lyre, flute and drums as instruments and began to play a slow, rhythmic melody to which the dancers crossed the hall. The tempo quickened, the ringing grew louder, and the heads of the audience nodded in time. Some clapped enthusiastically as the dancers leapt gracefully over the tables. Semiramis was happy to see Sargon's expression gradually start to relax. He still looked serious, but no longer as grim as at the start of the evening. After the last reprimand of his soldiers, they had not found an opportunity to speak to each other in private. On the journey to Nineveh, it had been easy to find a moment when they could talk without an audience. There in the city palace, all the walls had ears. She could not be too open with him lest she lose the trust of Nineveh's citizens. And while the war between their countries was fought far from Nineveh, the stories of the alleged atrocities of Sargon's men had, if anything, been made worse by that distance. *That my merchants are willing to put these things aside for the profits of trade is actually a success,* she thought, relieved.

In the garden, Senezon—by now quite drunk—took the lute from the hands of one of the musicians and launched into a drinking song. He was in an excellent mood. They had been served an outstanding wine to go with the roast venison, and it had quickly gone to their heads. The women laughed as the fighter tottered over to the musicians and took the instrument in his big hands. "Ezira, you're on the drum!" he commanded his friend. Ezira took a deep gulp from the wine goblet and joined him, and their song resounded loudly into the night.

The šagana had a well-tuned, sonorous voice, clear and melodic despite his drunkenness. The women clapped enthusiastically in time. The musicians, recovering from their initial surprise, began to accompany the Akkadian song. Ezira's drum set a fast rhythm that vibrated the furniture in the garden, and Gusur also threw himself into the songs of his homeland. The wine had overcome his reticence. He sang the refrain loudly and cheerfully, dancing between the couches. The women joined him, dancing and cheering on the singers. The servants quickly moved aside the tables with the food to protect the dishes from the merriment, but the wine continued to be poured. The singer's throat was large, as was his reserve of songs.

In the banqueting hall, Sargon heard his general singing as the entertainers took a break. A new course was served. With a smile, Semiramis said, "Hofileshgu and Woranola can count themselves lucky. Senezon is at his best tonight." She had noticed the group in the garden when she'd arrived. She raised her cup—like the plates, it was also made of blue glass. "Let us drink to the happy moments in life." Sargon, too, raised his glass and drank.

The wine was good and heavy. In Akkad, they had long ago begun to grow and press grapes. So far, however, they had not produced anything that was palatable without adding honey. The wine that was served to them today far surpassed anything the king had tried before. Earlier, Samše had explained that it was not from Nineveh, but came with the caravans from the Mediterranean. She seemed to have spent a small fortune to entertain her guests.

But Sargon could not shake off his suspicion that she had more in mind than just being the perfect hostess. So far, he had not detected anything to confirm his suspicions, and his tensions eased as the feast progressed. Samše enjoyed the appreciative words for her cooks' achievements and the astonished glances at the expensive crockery. The evening would be talked about in Nineveh for a long time to come and would be embellished more and more with each retelling. The queen had certainly made an impression when she entered the room, but that would pale against the memory of the banquet and the entertainment, and the singing šagana in the garden was a fresh addition to the night. Her steward had assured her that no overly expensive furniture or crockery could be broken out there. Enough wine had been provided. Everything was under control.

With dawn not far off, Semiramis decided it was time to bring an end to the celebration. She was the highest representative of Ishtar, and no guest would dare to leave before she did. She rose, thanked her hostess and the high priestess once more, and left the hall. Sargon followed her shortly afterwards and also made his way towards the palace, where his chambers were located.

In the garden, Senezon had grown into the role of leader of the group of šaganas. "Raise your cups!" he shouted, swinging his goblet aloft. "One more drink in farewell. We will never meet this young again!" He drained his wine in a single draught, and the others did the same. Hofileshgu led Ezira aside. "Take Senezon to your barracks with you. He would to better not to wander through Nineveh alone, not in this condition." The general nodded and hooked a hand under his friend's arm. "Up, great hero. It's time we gave our hostess back her garden."

"What for?" slurred the fighter. The wine had done its work. "They seem pretty comfortable over in their hole." But he put up no fight as Ezira led him to the gate. Woranola went ahead.

"Can you find your way to the camp?" Hofileshgu asked Gusur.

The prince nodded. "From here it's easy. I just follow the road to the Nergal Gate. From there I can see the torches at the camp." They said goodbye to their hostess and went their separate ways, Hofileshgu to the north barracks, Gusur towards the Nergal gate. His heart was lighter than it had been for a long time. The wine and the singing had intoxicated his senses. He thought he could still feel the warmth of Woranola's body—they had been very close when they danced. The scent of her skin still lingered in the air. For the first time, as he followed the long, deserted road, Gusur wished he could spend the night in the barracks rather than at the camp.

A few stars glimmered through the clouds as he passed through the temple district. Then, somewhere not too far away, he heard music and laughter. He looked up to the ziggurat, the white temple of Ishtar glowing against the deep blue of the sky. The square in front of the ziggurat was brightly lit, and music poured down to him from the topmost platform.

The wine and the lively evening had awakened his adventurous spirit. Without a second thought, he left the street and crossed the square in front of the sacred structure. His father had told them to get to know the city, hadn't he?

The square and the long stairway up to the temple were as empty as the road he had just left. There seemed to be people only on the uppermost platform. He could now

clearly hear the music coming from up there, mixed
with the bright laughter of women. He ran up the stairs
eagerly, two at a time. At the first platform, he paused
for a moment and looked out over the rooftops of the
sleeping city. In the distance he saw the signal lamps
atop the towers. On one side he could see the river following the city wall, on the other the rolling steppes
and distant mountains of Addad's realm. Somewhere
in between were his hunters. He had grown fond of
them, the courageous riders and their horses.

The sound of flutes and drums brought him back to
the moment. He ran up the remaining steps to the top
platform, following the alluring sound. Light radiated
from the great gates of Ishtar's white temple far into
the darkness. The house of heaven shone like the moon
on a starry night. The music and laughter were now
very close. The prince, curious, stepped through the entrance, out of the night and into the room, which was
bathed in glistening light.

What he found inside almost took his breath away:
women and girls in diaphanous white robes danced
wildly to the rhythm of drums and flutes, their bodies
coming together, writhing and rubbing, over and over.
Their mouths were open, their dark eyes large and ec-
static. The dancers were wearing very little, and their
breasts were bare or clearly visible beneath the sheer
fabrics. And there were those hands again, adorned
with delicate patterns that continued up their slender
white arms.

Gusur stood and stared at the spectacle as if in a
trance. Then he felt fingers gently caressing his shoulders and tracing down his back. More hands joined in,
stroking his arms and head. Delicate fingers ornamented with red drew him into the room and, almost hypno-

tised, he let himself be drawn. Hands found their way
to his chest and swept away his cloak. Someone guided
his left hand to a bare breast that nestled willingly beneath the pressure of his fingers. He felt the curve of
breasts on his back, too, while the fingers caressed his
body, stroking him as lightly as feathers from his chest to
his loins. The wandering hands found that part of him
that, at a touch, made him flinch with pleasure. He had
lost his willpower entirely and let the girls of the temple
guide him. Warm tongues brushed his chest and back.
He looked into the deep-brown eyes of a girl. It seemed
to him as if those eyes could peer into his soul, and he
sank into the dark pupils, so full of promise. He bent
and lifted the girl onto the altar behind her. Compli-
antly, she spread her legs as he pushed her flimsy robe
aside and caressed her small breasts with his hands.
Hungry eyes looked up at him expectantly. He held her
tightly, pushing forward deeply as she writhed beneath
him. Faster and deeper he thrust, as his sex overcame
her body's resistance. The girl moaned loudly.

Then, without warning, the music stopped, and angry shouts rang from the entrance. The high priestess
rushed into the room, followed closely by the temple
guards. Powerful hands tore Gusur away from the girl.
Semen and some blood flowed down his thighs and
dripped onto the floor, staining the light-coloured tiles.
A blow to the pit of his stomach made him double over.
Someone cried out. A woman? Another blow came,
this time to the back of his head, and he lost conscious-
ness. He fell to the ground and did not move.

The high priestess glanced contemptuously at the in-
truder who had desecrated the sanctuary. She sent the
musicians and dancers away. To the girl still perched
on the altar she said, "Wash yourself and have a doc-

tor examine you. We must see if he has damaged more than your innocence. Then come to my office!" To the guards she said, "Notify the governor immediately. Tell her what has happened. Then throw this bastard into a cell. I don't care what you do to him in the process but keep him alive until I have passed judgement."

She turned to her acolytes. "The rest of you clean the altar, now!" she snapped. "A disgrace like this in Ishtar's house. Disgusting."

Sargon marched gloomily through the streets of Nineveh to the temple district. The sun was high overhead and the houses cast only short shadows. The alleys were empty, as usual, the people shunning Marduk's light.

It had been reported to the king that one of his officers had been arrested for desecrating the temple of Ishtar. Who it was and what exactly had happened, the messenger had not known. The king had immediately sent for his šaganas, but he could not wait for them to report and had set off with two of his bodyguards. On another day, his god's light would have warmed his soul. Today it could not reassure him. What had happened? According to the messenger, judgement and sentencing of the man arrested would be passed by sunset. That seemed unusual for a people who otherwise conducted their business at night.

In the temple district, he turned into the house of the high priestess. Sentries stood at the gate, parasols protecting the soldiers from the glaring sunlight. Sargon told his bodyguards to wait for him there and he went inside alone. He was led politely but not warmly through the courtyard into the high priestess's reception room, where he was met by the murmur of many conversations. The room was filled with priestesses and representatives of the city council. He saw the governor talking vehemently with the high priestess, who was seated on a high chair next to a statue of Ishtar. The goddess was naked, the sculpture finished in white glass with rubies in her eyes, on her ample breasts, and between her legs. Gold chains adorned her neck, ears, and arms, and she wore a horned crown. One of the statue's arms was bent so that the palm faced upwards, as if the goddess were explaining something to him, the king thought. He bowed politely. The women interrupted their conversation, and the high priestess greeted him coolly. "I greet you, king of Akkad. You are late. We have already passed sentence on the desecrator. He is to be executed tonight."

Sargon's mind raced. Desecrator? Execution? What had happened? Where was Semiramis? Cautiously, he said, "Would the high priestess please be kind enough to tell me what happened to cause you to pass this sentence? All I have heard is that there was an incident in the temple."

"You should keep a better eye on your men," Samše hissed. "You obviously give them too much freedom, which they exploit to take advantage of the helpless. You should have known not to let this sex maniac loose on the city, alone, drunk. He invaded the temple and raped four virgins praying devoutly to our goddess." She looked up at the statue and bowed to it. The statue's red eyes seemed to glow in anger.

Sargon was puzzled. "There must be some misunderstanding, Governor. I know for a fact that Senezon was accompanied to the barracks by both Ezira and Woranola. He could not have molested your women."

"Senezon!" Samše snapped with contempt. "That lout couldn't have stuck his shaft in anything last night, not as drunk as he was. I'm talking about that one!" she said. She pointed to a corner, and Sargon turned to see Gusur lying between two guards, filthy and bleeding from many wounds. Sargon could hardly believe his eyes when he saw his son curled miserably on the floor. He walked over to him slowly and knelt down. The boy was conscious and looked up at his father with penitent eyes. The king laid a hand on his shoulder. *Why, Gusur,* he thought sadly. *Why have you done this?*

"My lord, please forgive me," the young man stammered, blood trickling from his mouth. "I have disgraced you. I don't know what came over me last night. They pulled me inside and I couldn't help myself."

"Liar!" the high priestess thundered. "Your lecherous eyes follow every skirt in the city. How many more of us have you screwed?"

"Only those who set their minds on it," Semiramis replied in a calm, firm voice. The queen was standing in the doorway. All eyes followed her as Ishtar's representative crossed to the image of her goddess.

"Are you defending the lawbreaker, Your Majesty?" the high priestess asked in horror. Semiramis met her gaze.

"Did he truly break the law? Or was he a victim?" she asked. She knew the rites of the Ishtar temple, where young women in service of the goddess willingly gave themselves to any man who desired them. At the moment of union, the lovers felt the goddess's supernatural power—the power of she who created everything, but also destroyed. The men who took part were generous donors, not only to the women, but also to the temple. Gusur, on the other hand, was to pay for taking part with his life.

Sargon was not prepared to abandon his son to such a fate. And he heard from Semiramis's words that she also doubted his guilt. The king straightened up and placed himself demonstratively in front of his son.

"Gusur is Akkadian, and I am his king. No one pronounces judgement on him but me."

"He must be stoned to death, in accordance with our laws," said the governor.

"Not while I live," Sargon replied and drew his sword.

"You dare threaten me?" cried the governor in feigned horror.

Semiramis saw it was time to intervene before the situation escalated even further. "The sword does not threaten you, governor. It is the symbol of the judge," she said with a smile. She stepped between them and addressed Sargon. "Take Gusur to your camp for judgement. Take all your men, too. The citizens of Nineveh are grateful that you want to fight with us against the enemies of the city. But before that, there must be no quarrel just because we do not follow each other's customs. From now on, I want your men to enter the city only when accompanied by our soldiers. The same will apply to any of our citizens who visit your camp."

Sargon wanted to protest, but Semiramis's steely look told him that she had pronounced judgement. He helped Gusur to his feet and together they left the house. Marduk's bright sunbeams shone on the Akkadians as they stepped outside. Their god was looking down on them, lighting their way.

Eighteenth Chapter:
The Alliance on the Brink

The king set down the clay tablet he was holding and looked around. A fire crackled in the centre of the tent, with cushions arranged in a circle around it, just as he liked it to be at home. Home. The word filled him with melancholy. They had been on the road for two moons now, first along the Tigris, then by ship to the north, and then almost four weeks in Nineveh, a city bigger than any he had ever experienced. And it was not only the streets that were convoluted, but also the connections between the traders, the written and unwritten rules of the city, and the influence of the temple and the city council, which was itself influenced heavily by the merchants. And then there were the endless documents, like the one that now lay before him. The king had read more clay tablets in the last four weeks than in the rest of his earlier life. Absolutely everything, it seemed, was written down here, including the orders for future military exercises. "When target strength has been restored and the new manoeuvres sufficiently practised, drills will be reduced to once a week," the tablet read. The word *once* was particularly deeply indented, as if the scribe had meant to emphasise it. *"The captains will assume supervision of their units and will assemble once every two weeks to report to the commander-in-chief. The town council will attend these meetings as needed."* Sargon had no doubt that the governor would decide when *as needed* would be without consulting him, so he would not find out what was really happening with the troops in the meantime.

The king read through the order on the clay tablet a second time, then sighed as he placed it on a small table. From the altar, the image of Marduk looked back at him. Sargon had unwrapped it on their journey only to pray, but in his rooms in Nineveh he had had an alcove emptied so that he could make offerings to be closer to his god. Now Marduk's eyes seemed to be scrutinising him. "Marduk, Lord! What am I supposed to do now?" he asked into the empty tent. "Anything can be done with this arrangement, anything except pitting the troops against each other. If an attack comes, the leaders will not understand their roles before Addad has already beaten us." The statue's serious eyes stared back at him. Sargon was the king. It was his job to carry out Marduk's will in the world.

He rang the bell. A servant entered and bowed.

"Where are Gusur, Senezon and Ezira?" Sargon asked.

"Prince Gusur has just returned from an inspection, Šagana Ezira is at the training grounds near the south barracks, and Šagana Senezon is in his tent." The king frowned. Why was the man sleeping during the day? Then he recalled that the city's infantry troops practised only at night. Senezon had kept to that rhythm even after their expulsion from the city. Sargon, however, had taken the opportunity to use the daylight hours again.

"I want all three of them outside my tent at dusk. It's about the latest defence instructions."

His men were already standing outside his tent when, towards evening, the king pushed aside the front flap and stepped out. On the horizon, far beyond the river and the endless steppes, Marduk's sun bathed the world once more in golden light. From the mountains to the north, Addad's clouds were already gathering to deny the people of Subartu the starlight and the moon of their goddess this night, as they had on all the other nights they had been there. Sargon felt sorry for the northerners and how their once-familiar sight was hidden from them. He, on the other hand, enjoyed feeling Marduk's power during Subartu's hours of daylight. He would climb a nearby hill and let his body soak up the sun's warm rays. Only in Akkad was Addad able to keep his clouds in the sky during the day. Here in the north he had to conserve his strength to veil the night from Ishtar's gaze. *It's good to know that even the powers of a god are limited,* Sargon thought.

Then he looked into the familiar faces of the men, who were looking at him expectantly. There was his oldest son, Gusur, who had had the misfortune to fall foul of the temple. He had since tripled his zeal. He personally checked every scout post daily and practised with every rider. As a teacher, he was blessed with endless patience and would one day become a great leader of his unit. Senezon stood impatiently, shifting his weight from one foot to the other. Big speeches—unless they were his own—and long waits were not his style. He embodied the war machine into which he was transforming his troops—leaving nothing to chance, optimised to the smallest detail, always deadly. That was the man, and that was how his soldiers were. Ezira led more by observation and advice. Nothing escaped his eagle eye. It was he who immediately spied the clay tablet in his king's hand. His eyebrows drew together.

"The council has decided that the city's troops have reached a satisfactory size and fighting strength," Sargon began the briefing.

"Satisfactory," snorted Senezon. "Satisfactory is far from good and much further from fit for war." In another situation, the king would have smiled at his šagana's wordplay. Today the situation was too serious.

"As a result, drills will be conducted only once a week in future, and the captains are to remain with their respective units."

Ezira was the first to voice concern. "They will unlearn all the teamwork we've just managed to put in place."

"And every one of those brave young things will start jumping out of line again, just to look extra brave," Senezon added. "Don't those peddlers on the city council understand anything?"

"I don't think the city council has ever had any desire to understand the point of our exercises," the king said. "That's what we soldiers are responsible for."

"Then they should let us practise as we see fit!" roared Senezon. "Otherwise we might as well drop the whole thing and go home."

There it was again, that word: home. "Is that what you want, Senezon?" asked Sargon. "Do you really want us to give Addad a free hand to attack first Nineveh, then the rest of Subartu and finally Akkad?"

"So far, the only been attacks we've faced have come from the councillors," the broad-shouldered šagana replied. "I don't think they like us helping them very much at all."

"So you say we should pull down our tents and leave the people here to their fate? Keep in mind: they will then do the same when Addad descends upon our tribes."

"He will have a much harder time with us than with the milksops here. All they care about are their hucksters and their money," Senezon said with conviction.

"And you, Ezira? What do you think?" the king asked.

"I lost two good men to the muskil when they raided our camp. Now Addad wants to lead them here and pass them off as *our* fighters. Here is where they will pay for their murders," Ezira replied.

"Gusur?"

"I have given my word to the hunters that I will fight at their side against Addad," Gusur said. "If you all want to go, then go! I will not go back on my word."

The king had expected this. The bond his son had developed with the Subartuan hunters was close. He made up his mind. "I'll pass our concerns on to the city council. While I don't expect it will make any difference, they have a weakness here for documenting every decision and statement. After that, I'll talk to Semiramis." *And then I will know if it's time for us to leave.*

In the palace, Sargon was made to wait before being allowed to see the queen. *This is unusual,* Sargon noted. In the past, Semiramis had put all other obligations aside when he had asked to speak with her.

Eventually, a man appeared. Sargon already knew him from their journey together from Akkad to Nineveh. "Queen Semiramis awaits you in the garden, Majesty."

The king nodded gratefully. When she wanted to be alone with her thoughts, Semiramis liked to retreat to the impressive gardens around the governor's palace.

The gardens were one of Subartu's many wonders that Sargon had come to know in Nineveh. Water was precious. In Akkad, if it was used for plants, it was only with the aim of producing food. In Nineveh too, numerous gardens growing vegetables and fruit lined the meandering Khosr. The palace gardens, however, served no useful purpose at all but existed only for the edification of the city's leaders. Flowering shrubs grew as tall as Sargon along the walls of the enclosure. Their fragrances caressed his senses. Gone all at once was the stench of the city, where the fumes of unwashed bodies, both human and animal, mixed with the dirt of the streets and the acrid smoke of the hearths. The desert heat, which radiated off Nineveh's walls deep into the night, was absorbed by the lush green of the lawns. Even the noise that never seemed to end in this city seemed to vanish in the trees. The king heard nothing but the singing of a few birds, the chirping of grasshoppers, and the rhythm of his own steps.

The gravel path he followed was lined with flowers that glowed in all the colours of the rainbow. Torches marked the path to a small lawn where he knew the queen would be.

He listened to his own footsteps on the smooth, round pebbles. Even these had been artificially laid here. With their light colour, they stood out clearly in the moonlight, so that even Sargon did not need a torch at night to find his way. If the daily hurly-burly of the merchants put the city's prosperity on display, that night it was the lush splendour of the garden that radiated Nineveh's wealth. Many tales had the desert king heard about the affluence of the sacred city. The reality surpassed them all.

He thought back over the many insights into the metropolis he had gained over the past weeks. There was the efficient, well-planned sewer system that served a population so large it took Sargon's breath away. Then there was the city administration: it had certainly been a wise decision to divide such a large city into districts, to keep order and collect taxes locally. Nor had the roads in Nineveh been left to chance but had been widened and sealed according to importance. This allowed the caravans to reach their destination as quickly as possible. Prominent stelae and fountains in the larger plazas made it easier for strangers to find their way. And everything was precisely recorded and kept in the huge archives for all eternity. So, despite the size of this metropolis, it was impossible for anything to escape the attention of the council, as Senezon had also had to accept during manoeuvres.

The manoeuvres. Here, too, the Akkadians had learned much that was new. The quality of the weapons in Subartu and the skill of the soldiers, especially of the women with their bows, exceeded anything he had seen before. Their lack of discipline and their self-seeking behaviour, however, mystified the king to this day. Senezon had once described it aptly by saying that Nineveh's units were more like a herd than an army. Yet he had trained them and over time had forged them more and more into a cohesive unit, despite the resistance from troops and councillors alike. Now the units were falling apart again—like the unity between the two kingdoms. Was it time to give up the experiment?

Sargon found the queen on a small stone bench in the middle of the lawn. Her bodyguards were positioned at a discreet distance, close but out of sight. Semiramis loved this place, where she could be alone beneath the canopy of her goddess's sky. In the simple, elegant dress she had worn when they first met in his tent, she ran her bare feet over the short-cut grass and looked at him with a smile. She looked like she had when she had waited in his tent to receive the welcome drink.

How much we've experienced together since then, Sargon thought as he approached.

Semiramis seemed to guess his thoughts. "Time passes quickly in your presence, Sargon. A woman would like to stop time, but you are always moving forward, always with your goal in mind."

"I wish what you are saying were true," he replied. "Everything seems to move in circles in Nineveh."

She smiled sympathetically. "But that's exactly what I meant. If we go round in circles, we can stay in place longer, but without standing still. We *do* move ahead, a little, but only when we have completed the circle. Like this, everyone can keep up."

"You've read the council's order?" It was more a statement than a question.

Semiramis sighed. "Samše took the opportunity to phrase the proposal in such a way that it would hit your honour hard. And that of your men. She would prefer to stop the exercises entirely and see you sail back to Akkad."

"And what do you want?" the king asked. His words came out more sharply than he'd intended. Semiramis, hurt by his tone, looked up at him. All at once her royal dignity was gone. A lonely woman looked up at the man who had come to support her in a city that was supposed to be hers. Sargon was stunned to see the fear in her eyes.

She stretched out her right hand to him, but he was too far for her to touch. "Sargon, please stay! Addad will roll over this city like a wave. We both know that. He is a master at pitting his enemies against one another. Ishtar and Marduk . . . even they did not realise his deceit until it was too late. Let us not make the same mistake, please!" she added, almost beseeching him.

The Akkadian said nothing, but he stepped closer and sat down slowly beside her, his gaze fixed on the distance. After a little while, he took her hand, which she still held out to him, in his, but he did not look at her.

"Gusur said to me earlier that even if everyone else returned to Akkad today, he would still stay. He has given his word to the hunters."

Semiramis thought of the young man and his passion for horses, which he shared with the hunters. She asked, "It's good to have a family you can rely on. Isn't it, Sargon?"

Her question took the king by surprise. Hesitantly, he said, "It's good not to have to doubt everyone's loyalty."

"Is it just loyalty? Isn't there more that binds you?" she said. When he did not reply, she continued, "At the temple, you were willing to accept any consequences to protect him. And he would do the same for you, at any time. Because you are family."

Again he was silent.

"It's good to have family, isn't it?" she repeated.

Now he answered with a question of his own. "What about you, Semiramis? Do you have family you can rely on?"

Semiramis looked up to where the moon shimmered behind the clouds. "I have a daughter, Ataliya. She bears the burden of ruling the empire one day. Her father died shortly after she was born. To this day, we don't know if it was an accident or if he was murdered. Since then, there has been only the two of us. Now Ataliya is at an age to start a family herself. She has never known a father or brothers. Because of that, I often wonder how she will find the right partner."

"Sanherib from your retinue impressed me greatly," Sargon said.

She nodded: "Sanherib will certainly make a good husband, but for someone else. He too had to grow up without a father or sister. I wish for Ataliya a husband who has that experience and who will hold together a family that supports her." She sighed. "We have too few good men in Subartu."

"Gusur has three siblings, all younger," Sargon replied. "The middle one is a sister, and she is at least as horse-crazy as her brother. He is her greatest role model." His mind wandered back to the day he had had to say goodbye at the camp. It felt as if years had passed since then.

Then, from the corner of his eye, he spied a game board on the bench on the other side of the queen. He had been surprised to discover, on their journey to Nineveh, that Semiramis also knew the equestrian game of the kings from the distant city of Ur, and they had played numerous games along the way. This time, white seemed to have a clear advantage over its black opponent. Two tokens symbolising horses were all that remained to be placed, and white had already taken three positions on its way to the royal court.

"Ig-na-til made a good start before she had to relieve the guard," Semiramis said, following his gaze. "Shall we finish the game?" Happy to accept the challenge—and to change the subject—the king moved to the other side of the board. Semiramis willingly let him play the white pieces, which clearly had the advantage. With the first throw of the dice, she reduced the lead to two to one, sending one of his leading horses back to the start. Sargon saw a chance in the open flank offered by the piece at the top of the board, but all the dice gave him was three points, too few to knock the piece back. He was left with a choice: either give up a strategic position on the board or start a new horse at the bottom. But down there, the chances of being beaten were greatest. True to his nature, Sargon stayed on the attack and placed the new horse. In the next round, the luck of the dice was once again on Semiramis's side. She still trailed two to two, but she had more pieces on the central file. Frowning, Sargon rolled the dice. He could not catch up with the black horses. In the end, Semiramis was the first to bring her pieces over the line.

"An early lead is no guarantee of a win," he sighed.

Semiramis nodded. "Nor does a single horse decide a game. If everyone sticks together, any advantage can be neutralised." She cleared the stones away. "Gusur is a good man," she noted. "Someday, the people of Nineveh will realise they misjudged him. And they will regret it."

Sargon nodded. "One day, they will also realise that they did not take their queen's warnings seriously enough," he said. "They will regret that too." After a brief pause, he added. "And when that happens, I want to be there."

A pale glow of light fell on them as a wayward wind dispersed the clouds for a brief moment, the moonlight shining on the stone bench where the king and queen sat. Semiramis breathed in deeply, absorbing the moment. New strength flowed through her body. She felt her back grow straighter, and the heavy burden she had borne since Sargon's departure from the palace dropped from her shoulders. *Let Addad plot his plots.* Ishtar was close to her.

Nineteenth Chapter:
Nineveh under Attack

The rider raced on towards his outpost. The guards there were resting, oblivious to the danger heading their way. The rider looked back constantly as he rode—he could not see his pursuers, but they had to be close. He spurred his horse onward, imagining he could hear the herd of fighting bulls at his heels. He could not see them, for the dense dust cloud billowing into a storm behind and around him made it impossible to see further than a spear's throw, and he prayed to Annuit that he was actually on the road to the city. Then the outpost appeared in front of him, the tent looming from the haze, the two guards jumping to their feet when they heard the hooves of the approaching horse.

"For Marduk to the north!" the rider shouted: the password. "Sound the alarm and ride to safety, now! An army's headed this way. Wild bulls are right behind me."

One of the guards lifted the heavy signal horn and blew two long notes. The blast penetrated the swirling dust, the sound reaching the distant city even as the rider raced on. He did not look back.

After he passed, the guards felt an eerie trembling underfoot, as if a giant were approaching with rapid steps. A rumbling grew from the opaque pall of dust that followed the rider, like the sound of boulders rolling down a mountain. The guards strained their eyes in the direction from which he had come. His hoofprints were still visible in the sand, but a pale haze blocked the horizon like a wall. But no, it was not pale everywhere. Dark patches appeared where the sky and earth met. They grew larger and blurred into each other, as if a dark cloud were rolling in between the sandy earth and eddying dust. Except that it was not a cloud.

"The bulls!" shouted one of the guards. He rushed to his horse, his comrade a second behind him. Their horses, still tied, were tugging wildly at their harnesses. In panic, they had long since realised the danger. The men struggled to untie them, losing precious seconds as the bulls thundered closer and closer, clearly visible now. At last, they managed to mount up. They turned the horses and spurred them towards the camp. But it was already too late. The impact of the charging bulls sent them flying from their saddles, and their horses were slashed by horns armoured with iron tips. Leaving their mangled bodies behind, the herd galloped on towards the camp of the unsuspecting Akkadians.

Sargon was outside his tent when he heard the warning from the outpost. He looked towards the hill to the east of the city and saw a rider galloping down the slope ahead of a wall of dust. He could hear a sound like thunder.

"Ezira!" the king shouted. Instantly, the general was with him. "Man the east bastion with the long lances!" This accursed area—they had not been able to find decent wood for barricades. The men hurried to their assigned positions, where archers joined them. The distant thunder was growing louder. Then the horseman reached the camp. He jumped off his horse and threw himself on the ground in front of Sargon.

"Bulls, sire!" he shouted. "Hundreds of them, driven by the muskil. Behind them is an army, too many for me to count. They're bringing heavy machines with them."

Then one of the guards shouted a warning and pointed to the hill from which the rider had appeared. Like a grim wave inside the sandstorm, an endless line of bulls now crested the hill. Sargon instantly discarded his plan to defend the camp. Their pathetic barricades would not stop that herd. Out here, against an enemy like that, the Akkadians had no chance at all.

"Retreat to the city!" he shouted. "Senezon, take the lead! Gusur, rearguard! If you're not already carrying something, leave it behind!" The soldiers abandoned their positions and ran for the city, although its gates had been closed since the Akkadians had moved out to their camp. Sargon estimated the distance to the gate, although he could no longer see it through the swirling haze, and the speed of the bulls charging down the hill. *Too far,* he thought grimly. *The bulls will be on us before we reach it.*

Inside the city, Semiramis was jolted from her sleep by a dream. It was early, the sunset still two hours away. Since the Akkadians had moved out of the city, sandstorms often swept the region during the day, hiding it from Marduk's eyes as well. If Addad could now control the day, too, it meant he was stronger than ever.

But something is different today. It's more than just a sandstorm, Semiramis thought, listening to the hazy world. The city rested peacefully beneath her palace window. She left her bed and stepped out of her chamber. A temple servant rushed to her immediately.

"What is it, Your Majesty?" she asked anxiously. "Are you unwell?"

Semiramis read the concern in the young woman's face and smiled reassuringly. "Nothing is wrong with me, Syczintia," she said and stroked an unruly strand of hair from the girl's face. Two guards had come up beside her in the meantime. She turned to them now and said, "I want to inspect the walls."

"You may be in danger outside, Your Majesty," one of them said. "Governor Samše has ordered us to protect you."

"Then you'd best come with me," she stated, irritated. The governor was restricting her movements more and more. Was it really only her distrust of Sargon and his men? Semiramis missed having Sanherib at her side. Her gal-ug would not have allowed anyone to try to constrain her. Only five of the loyal few who had accompanied her to Akkad remained. One of them was always close by, and now was no exception. "Mistinar, I want you with me, too," she said. With him beside her, she did not feel quite so much at the mercy of the two guards.

The small group climbed up to the broad wall walk that circled the city fifty feet above the streets below. Chariots stood ready to take them to the distant watchtowers on the north wall. Semiramis chose as her destination the tower that marked the outermost point in the northeast. The walls there pointed out to the camp where Sargon was now staying with his men. When they arrived, Semiramis ascended the steps to the tower and emerged unannounced—the queen was entitled to go anywhere in the kingdom, after all. Her small entourage followed. From the platform, she looked out in the direction of the camp and tried to make out the tents of the Akkadians. In vain. The swirling sand was too dense. *Strange days,* she thought. *Addad used to save his strength for the night. Why interfere during the day, when everyone but the Akkadians are asleep? Is he trying to hide us away completely? Or is he planning something bigger?*

"All is quiet there, Your Majesty," said a young woman of the guard to demonstrate her vigilance. "The desert foxes are keeping their distance from the city."

"As we asked them to," Semiramis muttered to herself. Somehow, that decision felt wrong today. Then the clarion call of a distant horn reached her ear. Two long blasts. She knew the sound, but not from her homeland. "Mistinar! Did you also hear that?" she said.

His furrowed brow answered her question even before he spoke. "Yes, Majesty. It came from the direction of the camp."

"You know the signal?" she asked him, to make sure she had heard it correctly.

"It is the Akkadians' warning signal. It comes from a great metal horn whose sound carries far."

"If it had been blown in the camp, it would have been louder," Semiramis said, weighing the distance to the camp and the effects of the dust cloud.

"Maybe the signaller was practising," one of the guards suggested with a shrug. "Or inside a tent."

Semiramis shook her head. The horn had sounded like a plaintive call from far beyond the camp. *No,* she thought. *This is not a drill.*

"King Sargon would never let his men practise with a horn like that on foreign soil. Sound the alarm!"

The certainty in her voice took the guards by surprise. Alarm? But Semiramis had made her decision. "Ugula! Alert the north gate. They must be ready to open at once. Danger threatens from the mountains, and we may need get King Sargon and his men behind the walls before the enemy is on them."

"Danger for the Akkadians, perhaps, but hardly for our city," said a voice from behind. Governor Samše had also stepped onto the platform and was slowly approaching the group. Two guards followed her.

So you've had me watched every step of the way, Semiramis thought. Aloud, however, she said, "If King Sargon is attacked, then Nineveh is also in danger. Addad's real target is our city, not his camp. Have you forgotten that?"

"Your Majesty, you have been talking about this ever since you arrived. And I have tried to explain that Addad has no reason at all to attack us. We have lived in peace for years. The only threat we face is from Sargon and his men. They probably tangled with some shepherds who are looking for revenge."

The scorn in the governor's voice was not lost on Semiramis. Samše seemed to be gloating at the idea that Sargon would waste his time with flocks of sheep. She made up her mind to reprimand Samše for that later. Now there were more important things to do.

"Governor Samše, in the name of the goddess I demand that you sound the alarm immediately. Open the gates and bring in the men from the camp!" Her voice had taken on an icy edge.

Samše was trembling with fury, but to refuse an explicit order would be treason. She bowed, her hands clenched into fists.

"As you wish, my queen. I will return to the palace and give the necessary instructions." With that she left the platform again.

"And hurry it up," Semiramis snapped behind her. Samše pretended not to hear.

Sargon stood between two tents, overseeing his soldiers' retreat. The Akkadians were now running back
towards the city, with Senezon and Ezira leading the
way. The bulls had already covered half the distance
from the crest of the hill and were coming faster and
faster after the retreating men. Sargon saw individual muskil galloping among the bulls. Most were armed
with bows, but some also carried swords. Sargon had
never realised so many of the centaurs existed.

"Father, you have to go now, too," Gusur urged him.

Armed only with his sword, Sargon knew his son
was right. There was nothing more he could achieve
here. Then a fireplace with a pot still hanging over it
caught his eye. "Fire, Gusur!" he cried. "Fire can turn
the bulls. Dump oil between the tents and set fire to it.
It will buy us some time, at least!"

Gusur understood. He grabbed a jug of oil and
poured a trail of the viscous liquid to the nearest tent.
A soldier did the same to the tent on the other side.
Sargon stood by the fire in the middle and waited until
they were done. Just as the bulls reached the outer tents,
he threw burning firewood into the trails of oil. A wall
of fire rose in front of him, engulfing the two tents. Sargon jumped back from the heat. The bulls in the front
row balked at the flames, and those behind, unable to
turn clear quickly enough, ran into them. Even some
of the muskil stumbled. The herd, panicked, ran in all
directions.

Thick smoke blocked the view, but the charge had
come to a halt.

"To the city!" Sargon shouted to the few still with
him in the camp, and the king of Akkad also ran for
his life.

"Fire in the camp!"

A shock ran through Semiramis at the guard's shout. The dust storm prevented a clear view, but it was clear that at least one tent was burning down below. She could also make out numerous shadows running through the sandstorm towards the city.

"It's the Akkadians!" she shouted. "We have to let them in."

The guards looked indecisively at each other.

"The gates are still sealed, Your Majesty," one said. "As you ordered, to protect the city."

Semiramis was horrified. Was she the only one in Nineveh willing to stand up for the men outside? Then no one would open the gates, no matter what carnage was being perpetrated out there.

"Mistinar," she said to the soldier who had travelled with her to Akkad. "Follow me to the gate!" She rushed down from the platform, leaving the relieved guards behind. None of them wanted to choose between the governor and the queen.

Outside, Senezon had reached the gate and was hammering at the heavy planks. "Wake up, you sons of bitches! Are you going to leave us out here to die?" There was no sound from inside. He looked around and saw Ezira approaching with his spearmen. "Where's the king?" Senezon asked.

"Still in the camp with Gusur. They stopped the bulls with fire, but it won't hold them for long."

"We won't last long out here either if these dozy hucksters don't open the gate right now."

Semiramis and Mistinar hurried down the tower and ran to the gate, where two guards were standing indecisively before the barricaded portal. From outside came the sounds of fists pounding at the wood.

"Open the gate!" the queen shouted as she ran.

One of the guards came towards her. "I am sorry, Your Majesty," the woman said. "The council's orders forbid us from opening the gates if danger threatens. Not without explicit instructions."

Before Semiramis could reply, Mistinar stepped forward and slapped the guard across the face. "You have your explicit instructions," he growled. The other guard did not resist. Together they raised the heavy crossbars that secured the gate.

Senezon was the first to notice the creaking of wood on wood. He and his foot soldiers were crowded in front of the gate, while Ezira and his spearmen formed the outer line. They did not have much to oppose the onslaught of the bulls, and they knew it. But now the gate opened. Senezon pushed his men through. "Be ready to close them up again," he bellowed, still outside. He looked towards his king, who was running for the sanctuary of the city with the remaining soldiers. But Senezon could see they would arrive too late—the bulls would be on them just outside the gate.

Beside him, Ezira had come to the same conclusion. Grim, determined, he picked up his spear and positioned himself to throw. His men followed his lead. "Senezon, get inside!" he snapped at his friend. "And see that your friend Woranola sends her archers to the walls, with all haste." Senezon had a retort on his tongue, but me merely nodded and disappeared through the gate. The thundering of the herd grew louder.

Sargon saw the open gate a short way ahead. Behind it they would be safe. He was running for his life, his guards close behind, Gusur bringing up the rear with a few stragglers.

A man stumbled beside the prince and fell to the ground. Gusur had no time to turn to see the man being trampled. Arrows whizzed past him from behind. Another man dropped to his knees, an arrow in his leg. The gate that would save them loomed larger and larger. He saw Ezira at the top of the ramp with his spearmen. They gauged the distance and hurled their weapons in unison. A wall of spears flew from the ramp, rising steeply into the air and flying over the heads of the fleeing men towards the bulls, even as the spearmen themselves quickly retreated inside the protective walls. A terrible bellowing filled the air as the spears found their mark. Bulls running behind stumbled over the carcasses in front, but not all were stopped.

Gusur realised that his father would not make it through the gate in time and he turned to face the herd. He managed to knock down two, but a third plunged a horn into his chest and spun him high into the air. The thunder of hooves was the last sound the prince of Akkad heard. Then he passed into the eternal void, a stranger in a strange land, but a hunter, too, who had found kindred spirits there in Subartu.

Inside, the Akkadians threw themselves mightily against the heavy gates when Sargon staggered through behind the last of his soldiers. The gates closed with a crunch and heavy crossbars crashed down into their brackets. Outside, the bellowing and blows gradually subsided.

Sargon looked around. Senezon was already shouting orders for the troops from the northern barracks to fall in. Ezira was on his way up the stairs with his spearmen. Gusur? The king could not see his son anywhere. Then Semiramis approached. "Gusur did not make it to the gate," she said gently. "A bull caught him before he reached the ramp."

Gusur . . . is dead? The thought struck Sargon like a slap. Impossible! He scanned the ranks of survivors once more. His son was not among them. Gusur? Then the terrible certainty crept into him like the icy cold of the night. Dead? He looked around a third time, hoping against hope that he had somehow overlooked his son. Then his eyes met Semiramis's, and he saw her pity and sorrow. The truth wrapped him in its grip like a giant fist. *Gusur is dead.* He staggered. The weight of his sword dragged his right arm to the ground, as if to tell him: let go, it's over! A thousand eyes seemed to be staring at the king. All he wanted was to be far away, alone. Gusur? Suddenly, he felt very old. What am I doing here? What's the use of all this? The cold filled every fibre of him. Dark thoughts flashed through him like ghostly shadows. He could not move. As if turned to stone, he stood in the midst of his soldiers while the wild shouts of the attackers rang beyond the gates.

Semiramis watched the change in him with concern. She stepped closer and spoke urgently. "Sargon, Gusur saw his father make it. He saw you get through the gate safely. He died knowing that you would live."

With an effort, Sargon turned his face to the queen. His eyes wandered over her creased, worried brow until they were magically drawn to the depths of her eyes— the deep blue of the night sky flashed through him.

Semiramis gazed deep into him. She saw inside him the sadness, felt how numb he'd become. She gathered all her energy, directing it into her gaze as she had done when they first met. But this Sargon was a different man. Gone were the searing rays of the sun, the burning eyes that had almost knocked her off balance back then. This Sargon was as cold and wasted as a tree deprived of water. The queen took a deep breath and began to draw his gaze into the depths of the night, towards the water she knew he needed. Sargon could not take his eyes off her. He tried to fight her off, weakly, but she did not let go. Her thoughts settled softly over his wounded heart, each one like the gossamer garments that clothed the queen. His resistance faded further. She drank in his gaze, deeper and deeper. Then Sargon discovered something else. In the darkness of her eyes, a star sparkled, followed shortly by a second. His curiosity was aroused, like that of a small child. He let Semiramis lead him, unresisting now, into the depths of the night, into the realm of Ishtar. Soon, he no longer perceived anything in the darkness, except for tiny, twinkling stars. They formed themselves into images and symbols.

Everything was strange, but nothing was threatening to the Akkadian. He felt light, as if his body were being carried gently along by a stream. From a distance, he heard a whisper: "Live, Sargon! The living need a living leader now. Leave the dead to the gods." Sargon could make out no one in the darkness. Semiramis? "Live Sargon! Leave the dead to the gods." The voice grew louder. Sargon felt himself lifted, felt his journey leading him back from the realm of Ishtar to the world of humans. "Live Sargon!" rang loudly in his ear.

Then the king realised that his eyes were closed. He opened them and found Semiramis's face close over his. Her gaze had taken on a chill aspect, iron-like, like the sheen of the drawn sword in her hand. Muffled pounding against the city gate and bellowing from the besiegers outside the walls finally brought the king back to the moment. He shook himself physically, vigorously, shaking off his heavy thoughts like the dust of the desert after a long journey. From underneath, the sunfire of Marduk streamed again through every vein of his body. Ezira was still on the stairs to the watchtower and Sargon called up to him, "Ezira! Stay behind the barricades with your men. Watch out for their archers! The bulls can't harm the walls. Save your ammunition for the army behind them." The general turned and confirmed the order with a nod.

"What army?" Semiramis asked.

"The scout reported that the bulls were only the vanguard. An army with siege engines is following from the north." To a group of guardsmen he said, "Send the archers here, on the double. And tell Hofileshgu to get her soldiers to their catapults. Then bring plenty of water to soak the roofs of the houses near the wall." The men hurried off to carry out their orders.

In the meantime, all of Nineveh was awake. People were running through the streets as news of the attack spread, and the curious were already flocking to the gate—they wanted to see the muskil with their own eyes. Senezon had to post guards to keep them from climbing the stairs. Sargon ascended the tower beside the city gate. He found Ezira at the top, peering intently into the surroundings.

"You can hardly see anything through the sand," Ezira said. "But they seem to be retreating from the walls."

"Where are they now?" asked Sargon.

"There! Look!" cried a man, pointing to the west. In the distance, in the light of the setting sun, they could see dark shadows moving along the city walls towards the river.

"The villages," Sargon growled. "They're attacking the villages by the walls." He ran down from the platform with Ezira and west along the wall walk to the western wall.

The bulls and the terrible creatures driving them were rampaging through the tents and huts between the great city walls and the river. Any men, women, and children unable to escape to the other bank in time were trampled or slain. The sound of screams, timbers breaking, and animals wailing merged with the galloping hooves, creating a strange melody that rang even inside the walls of Nineveh. The soldiers on the battlements were helpless. They could only watch the cruel spectacle taking place between them and the river.

In the barracks, the alarm signal jolted Woranola from sleep. *An attack?* she wondered, dressing hurriedly. On the parade ground, her archer units were ready and waiting. Then the governor appeared. Her garments were reinforced with metal plates, and she wore a helmet and boots like a soldier. Several guards followed close behind her.

"War bulls!" she shouted to Woranola from afar. "The muskil are driving them through our villages by the river. They're destroying everything. You have to stop them at once!"

"Where is the king?" asked the gal-ug, keeping her wits about her despite the danger.

"Safe with his soldiers at the north gate," the governor replied. "The bulls have already moved on. They're running amok through the villages here. You have to stop them before they destroy the new docks, too. Now!"

The young woman hesitated. Officially, King Sargon was still commander-in-chief. She had clear instructions to take orders only from him. But he was in the north of the city, and she had not yet had any orders from him. She made her decision.

"Hatuti!" she snapped, calling over a woman from the first unit. "Go and tell King Sargon that we are on the western walls in the southern part of the city. We will fight the bulls from there. Tell him to send us the spearmen. We can fight them together."

"It will be too late for that!" cried the governor. "They won't get here from the north gate for an hour. By then the docks will be gone. We must act now."

"Governor," Woranola said firmly. "If we are really up against Addad's bulls and the muskil, our archers have no chance. In the open field, with no cover from ground troops, they will be slaughtered."

"You won't be unprotected," the governor said vehemently. "As you can see, I have my two personal units with me."

The young woman eyed the troops for a moment. "Two units, only one with spears," she said. "The muskil will have an easy time of it."

"I see," the governor replied, suddenly cool. "You are afraid of facing a real opponent for a change. Our city is clearly in need of better leaders." She strode demonstratively past Woranola to the leader of the first unit. "Zickla! I am sure you will not let our citizens down."

Zickla's eyes sparkled. She went down on her knees. "What are your orders, Ma'am?"

"I hereby appoint you Šagana Lú Ti, commander-in-chief of all archers in Nineveh. Let us drive back these savages together."

Woranola stepped forward. "Governor, with all due respect, our queen has designated King Sargon to select officers. We owe him our allegiance."

"The desert fox is lucky to even be alive. His men were hopelessly outmatched. What use is he to us? We should never have let them join our ranks." To the leader of the first unit she said, "Zickla, I ask in the name of the council: what are your instructions, Šagana Lú Ti?"

Suddenly promoted to the rank she'd always wanted, the ambitious young woman hesitated. Against bulls and muskil, her archers were highly vulnerable. The bulls would be on them before they were even out of the gate.

"Woranola!" she began gruffly, to cover her uncertainty. "Take units five to nine. Cover us from the walls above the barracks gate. I'll take my unit and units two, three, and four with me. Units ten, eleven and twelve will form the reserve. We'll get even with those butchers."

In the meantime, Hofileshgu and her units had arrived at the north wall. With her troops moving their defensive machines into position, she went to see King Sargon, who had moved with Queen Semiramis to the watchtower at the western end of the north wall. The sandstorm had abated somewhat, but the sun had now set, and clouds again covered the night sky. Dark smoke rose from the villages along the river. Queen Semiramis stood at the battlements a few steps away, trying to see the huts where the bulls still raged, and where men, women and children were dying. The king, however, was looking in the other direction, towards the mountains. Hofileshgu, beside him, followed his gaze but could not see anything out of the ordinary.

"The bulls are just the beginning," the king said. "Addad is not here to frighten us with children's games." His words brought Semiramis out of her thoughts. She turned and came up beside him, and Hofileshgu went down on her knees before her. With a gesture, Semiramis invited the gal-ug to stand and say what was on her mind.

"Your Majesties, what is happening? What will become of us?" Hofileshgu asked.

It was Sargon who spoke, but it was clear that the queen shared his thoughts. "The bulls are a distraction," he said. "They want us to withdraw our troops from the walls. His army will soon emerge from the sandstorm. I expect them to attack at the north gate."

Hofileshgu looked around. "Where are Woranola and her archers?" she asked.

"I've sent for them. They should be on their way."

Just then, a scream came from one side.

"Your Majesty, there!" yelled a guard, his eyes fixed on the north. Sargon hurried to the battlements but could see nothing. The people from Subartu had better eyes.

"They are coming," Semiramis stated flatly.

Hofileshgu said, "I count four siege towers. Your Majesty, we have only three catapults to the north. I fear at least one of their towers will reach the wall."

"Then make sure there are no more," Sargon replied, tightening the buckle on his helmet. "We'll take care of the one that gets through."

Hofileshgu hurried down from the platform to her units. Where the hell was Woranola?

Urta gently patted her horse's neck. The sandstorm was abating now, and the beast sensed the danger Urta could make out in the distance. Her companions also looked on grimly as the bulls destroyed the Akkadian camp. *Prince Gusur is there too,* she thought in despair. *And we're just sitting out here watching.* They could see the musk-il, the supernatural half-man, half-horse creatures spoken of by the ancients. As a child she had been afraid of them. Later she had consoled herself with the thought that they probably didn't exist at all and only ruled the steppes in legends. Now she saw for herself that the legends were true.

Urta and her companions had been resting at the southern outpost before their scouting foray. When they heard the alarm signal, they immediately set off together. The bulls had approached incredibly fast and quickly cut off their route to the camp. The hunters had then turned back and ridden out into the steppes, circling in a wide arc around the herd. They spotted Addad's army just in time, following the bulls in a cloud of dust. Tall, wooden, ox-drawn siege towers rumbled towards the walls of Nineveh. Sturdy warriors with axes and spears marched behind the machines in the pale light of the setting sun. Never before had Urta seen an army so big.

Then they were seen. Units of swift spearmen galloped towards the hill from which she and her companions had been watching the spectacle. Urta and the other hunters escaped well before the thunder god's fighters were within striking distance, galloping south into the night. No one followed them—the attack was focussed on Nineveh. When they were clear, Urta signalled her group to stop.

"Irgigi, Telal, ride to the woods and gather all the hunters you can find. We'll meet at the city wall, south of the Khosr."

In the meantime, the governor's two units had re-formed at the barracks gate. They were ready to strike out. Samše stood before them and issued her final instructions to the new šagana of the archers.

"We form a phalanx between the bulls and the dock. The dock is higher than the shore. You and your archers will take positions there. The reserve will be on the ramp in front of the gate. With the units on the wall, you attack the beasts from behind."

"Can we use flaming arrows?" asked Zickla. "They could make the bulls panic."

"Too dangerous," the governor said. "The huts are made of straw. They would burn down completely." The newly appointed šagana wanted to point out that the huts were already lost but thought it better to hold her tongue. Samše had not taken kindly to Woranola contradicting her.

At the governor's command, the gates opened. Samše and her units marched out, the archers following close behind. From the huts, people ran towards them in panic. Samše let them pass to get to the safety of the city. She herself stayed just outside the gate with the reserve archers. Zickla and the rest of the archers, meanwhile, hurried to the dock. Nothing could be seen of the bulls in the darkness and the thick smoke that swallowed the huts. Only the vibrating earth underfoot told them they could not be far away. They reached the dock unhindered. So far, it was still undamaged and jutting proudly into the river. Rowers on boats were preparing to cast off to safety on the far side. Zickla's archers grabbed barrels and baskets, whatever they could use to build a bulwark to the north, behind which they could entrench themselves.

Then the bulls came. Huge, black beasts, their horns wide and dangerous. They rolled towards the archers like a dark, deadly wave. But there was no sign of the muskil.

Zickla called to her archers to wait for her signal. But just as she raised her arm, an archer beside her collapsed, two arrows protruding from her back. Startled, Zickla spun around. From the south, the centaurs came charging in. Their arrows felled the archers on the dock before most could even turn. Simultaneously, the herd of bulls closed from the other side, trampling the governor's troops on the wooden dock, which gave way with a crash. None of those who had gone out returned to the city alive.

Woranola could only watch helplessly from the wall as the troops on the dock were slaughtered. Addad had allowed the storm to subside as if to show them the horror he intended for the city. The river was just out of range of their arrows, and while they killed a few bulls, what did that count against the losses they suffered on the riverbank?

She brought back the governor and the reserve archers from the ramp in front of the gate and had it secured. No one else emerged from the ruined huts, and the bulls pushed on to the fields of grain that lay south of the road. Woranola counted their losses—about half their numbers had died for this senseless failed manoeuvre. Grief and anger seized the young woman, and for a moment she thought about going out herself to take revenge. Then a man she knew from their joint exercises ran up to her, drenched with sweat and trembling. He had obviously run a long way as hard as he could.

"Ma'am!" the man began. How strange it sounded to her to hear this salutation so naturally again, having been deprived of it just a short time before. "King Sargon needs you and your units at the north gate immediately. A siege army is approaching." Startled, Woranola looked across the rooftops of the city towards the distant north gate. Signal fires had been lit there, and smoke from burning buildings rose in the distance. The enemy was already at the walls, and again she was too far away to do anything about it.

The messengers reported to Urta about events around the walls. Thirty-six hunters had already arrived, and more were coming in.

"The muskil and their bulls are now at the south gate," the man reported. "They've destroyed the villages along the river."

"What are the people in the city doing?" Urta asked.

"They could not stop the bulls. Their soldiers were routed at the new dock—I saw it myself. There are archers on the battlements, but the muskil are staying out of range."

"Why are their archers in the south at all?" she asked in amazement. "Isn't the main attack in the north?"

"Maybe they haven't realised it yet," the man speculated. "Nineveh is big. It can take time for the orders to reach the barracks."

"We have to warn them," Urta said. She ran to her horse. "We ride to the Shamash Gate. It's only a short way from there to the barracks gate. If the archers don't get to the north wall, Nineveh is lost."

Gal-ug Hofileshgu completed her inspection of the defensive catapult. She was satisfied. She and the others there were ready. She had given clear instructions as to which of the catapults was to attack which of the four siege towers the attackers had brought. For now, Hofileshgu had decided to ignore the one farthest to the north. If it got through, they would stop the attackers on the walls. She herself took charge of the machine between the north gate, through which Sargon had reached safety with his men, and the Halahhu Gate, at the outermost tip of the north wall. Her target was the tower closest to the city, so the first shot was hers. She had to be on target, no matter what. A miss would unsettle the others.

She calculated the distance to her target a final time, then gave the signal. The arm and basket carrying the boulder shot skyward. In a high arc, the stone flew over the wall and the closer troops and slammed into the main body of the siege tower. Its supporting beams destroyed, the high tower collapsed. Screams and crashes came from outside the walls, and the soldiers at the catapult cheered. Hofileshgu let out the breath she'd been holding as the stone flew towards its target. Then she and her unit hastily set to reloading the machine before the fourth tower drew too near. But she knew there was not enough time.

The artillery leader at the machine south of the north gate had cheered loudly when her gal-ug destroyed the tower. Now it was her turn. Her target was approaching along the road to the gate. *It is almost an insult to approach the city so indifferently*, she thought. She had practised countless times against targets on the road and did not doubt for a moment that she would hit the tower. She cast a last appraising glance at her target, made a slight last-second realignment, then gave the order to fire. The arm crashed against the crossbeam and the boulder flew towards the siege tower. At first it seemed it would narrowly miss its target . . . but no, it smashed through the planking and supports on the south side. The archers' platform at the top tilted, then crashed down onto the troops advancing beside the tower, the debris blocking the road for the following troops.

The platoon leader at the third machine saw with satisfaction that the other two had destroyed their targets. He was the only man among the officers and had the most difficult task of all. His catapult was at the Nergal Gate, far from the attackers. He had to let his target get closer to the walls to be in range. The archers atop the tower had long been within shooting distance and were shooting flaming arrows into the city even as he made the final adjustments.

"Fire!" he shouted, and he prayed silently to Ishtar that his aim was true. The heavy projectile flew along the walls towards its target and struck the siege tower low, near the wheels. The impact was hard enough to smash through the shields and several supports. The tower tipped sideways and toppled onto the desert sand, sending up a cloud of dust. Furious screams rang out from the fields outside the city. The men and women at the catapults cheered and embraced each other.

But there was still one tower to the north, moving unimpeded towards the city.

Twentieth Chapter:
The Walls Come Down

Hofileshgu gave up trying to get the machine ready to fire again. It was simply taking too long. The leader of the remaining tower seemed to realise that Nineveh's defensive catapults would no longer be reloaded in time, and he steered the tower a little further south, heading for a section of the wall that seemed easier to breach.

Hofileshgu turned and peered to the south, hoping to finally see Woranola and her archers. Then the defensive machine on the eastern wall caught her eye. It was about three hundred metres south. Suddenly, she knew how she could stop the fourth tower. Without hesitation, she jumped from the catapult and called to her unit to follow her. They hurried along the walls, staying low behind the battlements to avoid the arrows flying overhead. With no attack threatened from the east, the catapult on the east wall had been left uncrewed. Together, Hofileshgu and her unit turned the heavy frame and aimed the machine to the northwest, towards where the tower was approaching.

"Ma'am," a woman beside her said, keeping her voice low. She had served for a long time and could see what Hofileshgu had in mind. "I hope you know what you are doing. It is too far. From here, we are more likely to hit the wall than the tower."

Hofileshgu nodded grimly and replied, "Not if we lighten the stone. Cut it down by a quarter. That should be enough." The woman immediately set to work with hammer and chisel. Hofileshgu knew she could rely on her.

Together the women heaved the trimmed boulder into the basket. Hofileshgu estimated the distance. The tower was almost at the wall, and the troops on top were already preparing to swing a trapdoor over as a gangplank to cross onto the battlements.

"Ishtar with us! Fire!" shouted the gal-ug. The rock was hurled high by the machine and hurtled towards the wall. It flew just over the battlements, missing them by a hair's breadth, and smashed through the open trapdoor. It penetrated deep inside the tower. Even cut by a quarter, the heavy projectile had lost little of its destructive power. The tower's framework buckled, and it fell—this one, too, did not reach its destination.

From his vantage point above the city gate, Sargon observed the defence with growing confidence. The penetrating force of the defensive machines and the skill of their units impressed the king greatly. After losing their last tower, the attackers retreated from the wall and instead set to clearing the wreckage from the road to the north gate, opening a path for the battering rams. *Where are the archers?* Sargon thought. *Woranola should have been here by now.*

New war machines appeared behind the besieging troops. These were smaller than the siege towers, and each had a round turret on the roof and carried a heavy beam suspended horizontally that swayed in time with the steps of the soldiers pushing them. A heavy iron weight protruded at the front. "Battering rams," Semiramis said grimly. "Addad knew our catapults could not be reloaded quickly. The siege towers have cleared a path for the rams to break the walls." Nineveh's defenders could only watch helplessly as the mighty rams rolled closer.

At the same time, Urta and her hunters entered at the city gate and galloped down the long road to the barracks gate. No one tried to stop them. The hunters were well known from the competitions that had been held every week in honour of Annuit. Urta and her unrivalled horse were now famous throughout the city. People cleared the way when they heard the sound of galloping hooves. When she reached the barracks gate, Urta leapt from her horse and raced up the steps to the platform atop the watchtower, where she believed the leaders of the archers had to be. As she climbed the last steps, she saw Woranola gazing north to where the main attack was underway.

The young gal-ug turned at the sound of Urta's quick steps on the stairs. She knew the famous huntress. Prince Gusur had introduced them after the first competition. But instead of a greeting, Urta called out: "Addad is attacking! You must get to the north gate at once!"

Woranola nodded. "I received the same message from King Sargon just now. Addad has made fools of us. He used the bulls to keep our archers in the south."

"How soon can you get to the north gate?"

"If the roads are clear, in half an hour."

"And if they're not?" asked the huntress. "The road to the Weavers Well is choked with people fleeing this way."

Woranola thought for a moment. "We can bypass that road, but we will lose time." Senezon's experience was still fresh in her mind, a cautionary tale.

The huntress looked to the north, where the smoke from burning houses was growing thicker. Then she turned to the city wall itself. "Is the wall walk as wide everywhere as it is here?" she asked.

"Yes it is," the gal-ug replied hesitantly. "But it will take even longer up here. "

"But it's empty," the huntress replied.

"Even so! If we follow the wall, it will take us over an hour just to reach the Nergal Gate from here. And the battle is even further north."

"Not if we take the horses," Urta said. "Divide your people into two groups. We have forty riders. Each of us can take one of you. One group will take the west wall, the other the east wall from Shamash Gate. As soon as we drop the first of you, we'll come back for the others. Let's go!" Together they ran from the watchtower down to the wall walk.

The battering rams pounded like thunder against the wall. The few archers on the wall could do little against the mighty machines. Again and again, the heavy, iron-tipped pole swung back and was hurled against the wall with great force. Another ram was already attacking the timbers of the north gate. Inside the wall, Sargon had divided his soldiers into three groups to face the enemy when the walls fell. Senezon was with his infantry units south of the gate, while Ezira and the spearmen prepared their defences at the gate itself. The king himself led the defenders to the north, where the largest force was expected to break through. Semiramis had also donned armour. With sword and shield, she stood alongside Sargon. Acrid smoke rose from the houses behind her.

"It was once prophesied that I would meet you on the battlefield," Sargon said. "At the time, however, I thought we would be fighting against each other, not side by side."

"Oracles are notoriously difficult to interpret, but they are always true." She held out her hand and he took it in his.

"You are a formidable woman and a wise queen," he said. "It has been an honour to lead your troops."

She smiled, and in her eyes Sargon once again saw the glittering depths of the night sky.

"We are not finished yet, Sargon. Addad was wrong when he thought he could pit us against each other. Now let him be wrong again if he thinks Nineveh is defenceless."

The iron-tipped ram penetrated the city wall with a crack, and heavy chunks of brick came crashing down. The battlements high above slumped, forming a crater that took more of the wall with it. Jubilant shouts rang from outside. Sargon was standing in the midst of his troops, opposite the breach in the wall. More and more sections were broken out until there was a breach about three metres wide. A warrior wearing a horned helmet and a shaggy fur appeared in the opening. Swinging his axe high, he bellowed his battle cry into the city. Hundreds of throats behind him took up his call, and the walls literally shook. Sargon gripped his sword tighter and charged at the breach. Semiramis and her soldiers followed close behind. Then the king heard a distant whistling sound that rapidly grew louder. Sargon knew only one person whose arrows sang that sound.

Nintinugga? thought the baffled king. *Gods, are you playing with my senses? Am I dreaming?* The whistling grew louder and louder until all at once it stopped. The warrior with the horned helmet flinched, then fell headlong into the city through the breach in the wall, an arrow protruding from his neck.

On a rise far behind the attackers stood a slender figure on a chariot. She raised her bow high. The charioteer beside her kept the horses steady. More chariots appeared on either side until they spanned the entire hill. Mari's army had arrived in Nineveh.

It had taken some effort to lead the horses up the long steps to the battlements, but now they were galloping north atop the long walls. Woranola wrapped both arms around Urta as the huntress spurred her horse to a hard gallop. As she rode, the huntress blew her horn to disperse the guards posted along the way. Passing the Mashki Gate, they could now see not only the smoke billowing ahead of them, but flames, too. The attack was concentrated on the wall between the three northern gates.

"Lead us to the Nergal Gate!" Woranola ordered. Urta nodded.

They turned the corner onto the wall walk along the north wall. Woranola could now see the attacking troops for the first time. The sheer size of the enemy army took her breath away. Nineveh had never been attacked by such a massive formation. The city's ground troops would be hopelessly outnumbered in the open field. *But we are not in the open field,* the gal-ug thought grimly. At last they reached the towers at the Nergal Gate. Woranola jumped down and ran up the steps to the platform above the north tower. Her unit followed.

Urta and the other hunters were already racing south again to pick up the next fighters.

The young woman took the steps up the narrow stairway two at a time. On the platform, however, she forced herself to slow down and get her pulse back under control. Three archers were already on the battlements, and they greeted the reinforcements with joy. Woranola looked down at the wall between them and the next gate. A battering ram stood close to the gate, its heavy pendulum slamming into the stone wall over and over. Cracks were already forming on the wall walk. Just inside the wall, she could see several units of the city guard. Senezon was leading them—the young woman recognised his stride and posture immediately. *Addad's troops are in for a surprise if they thought they only had to get through the walls,* she thought. But she didn't want to let it get that far. Her archers were already burning oil for flaming arrows.

"Concentrate on the ram," she ordered. "They can't get through without it." Arrows rained down on the heavy vehicle, but it had been reinforced with heavy metal plates. The burning arrows ricocheted off or stuck ineffectively in its armoured shell. The attackers now noticed the increased danger threatening from above. Waves of arrows flew high and fell on the platform, forcing Woranola and her troops to take cover. The heavy ram pounded unceasingly at the city wall until finally a section of the wall broke with a crash and collapsed.

The battering ram methodically widened the hole in the wall, heedless of the arrows flying down from above. Finally the gap was wide enough. The heavy wagon was hauled back to clear the way for the invading troops. The archers immediately changed their ammunition and took aim at the troops who, covered by large shields, were now advancing towards the breach in the wall.

Down below, Senezon had seen the increased fire from the tower, and he waved up gratefully to Woranola. As soon as the battering ram was withdrawn, he charged with his soldiers into the gap to intercept the attackers there. Nineveh's soldiers formed a wall of shields and swords, as he had taught them, and the endless exercises that the stocky Akkadian had demanded of them paid off. No one jumped out of line or broke from their place. Each one covered the next fighter, and if one went down, another immediately took their place. Woranola's archers now concentrated their fire on the rows immediately in front of the defenders, causing the attackers to raise their shields overhead, exposing themselves to Senezon's forces. The fallen attackers hindered the troops behind them, and the attack quickly came to a near standstill.

But there were still many, many enemy troops outside Nineveh. Sooner or later, the last defender would fall. *Not while I still live*, thought Woranola. Another unit of archers arrived, with fresh supplies of arrows. Below them, the ground turned red with the blood of the fallen.

Ezira, however, had no archers to help his unit against the battering ram at the gate. The defenders could only watch helplessly as the battering ram was slammed again and again against the heavy timbers. Outside the city, Addad's horsemen were ready to enter Nineveh. *Will they use the bulls again?* Ezira wondered, but a loud cracking noise snapped him out of his thoughts. The armoured tip of the ram had smashed through the gate and now loomed menacingly through a gaping hole.

Further blows destroyed the wooden gate completely. Ezira did not hurl his spear at the battering ram—a simple spear could not harm the iron-clad machine. As soon as the battering ram was withdrawn, his soldiers immediately filled the gap created. Arrows assailed the defenders, but struck only their large shields, between which their spears protruded. Then Addad's horsemen attacked, the warriors driving their mounts towards the wall of shields and spears. Shouts, snorting, and the clash of iron on iron echoed into the night. Again and again, Addad's horsemen charged Ezira's soldiers, who stood their ground, firm and courageous. But Ezira saw his numbers slowly dwindling, while the waves of horsemen charging the gate seemed endless.

All at once, however, the attackers broke off. Arrows continued to fly, but no more horsemen appeared. Ezira was too wary to believe the battle was over.

Then a man called from the watchtower above the gate. "Šagana Ezira, help has come from the mountains!"

Ezira instantly left his place at the gate and climbed up to the observation platform, where the man was pointing excitedly to the northwest. On the hill behind the attackers, the šagana could see a long line of chariots. The attackers had also seen the arriving reinforcements, Ezira realised, and were reforming, the horsemen taking up positions on both flanks. The attack to the northeast of the gate, where his king and Semiramis commanded the defence, had also come to a halt. Senezon seemed to have the situation at the wall to the west of the gate under control. Ezira now saw the archers on the towers of the Nergal Gate, and more were arriving just then to support his spearmen. They rushed up to the towers to occupy the battlements.

"Hold our position," he called down. "And watch out for their arrows! Tell the workmen to get the new gate in place, now!"

From the hill, Nintinugga watched the attackers break off their attack on the walls and turn towards them. Sanherib smiled at her.

"If you ever felt parched for attention, my love, that thirst should now be well and truly quenched."

"It's nice to hear your concern for my feelings. But I'd much rather have you looking at me than what's heading our way down there."

It had been more than a week since they had left Mari for Nineveh. At first they had followed the Khabur river upstream to the old city of Chagar Bazar, which lay close to the border of Semiramis's realm. Few people still lived in the once great city, but the travellers were able to replenish their supplies before setting off through the desert to the Tigris. They reached the river in two days and crossed at Tarbisu. The people there had fled their homes in panic when they saw the army of desert fighters approaching. Sanherib, however, had eventually managed to convince them that they were on their way to help Nineveh. Horses and soldiers alike had taken the opportunity to refresh and fortify themselves before moving on to Nineveh, and the governor of Tarbisu, to avoid more such incidents, had given him a standard that bore the coat of arms of Subartu, which Sanherib had attached to his chariot.

That standard now fluttered in the wind as Addad's troops formed up in front of them. Their vanguard consisted of a phalanx of spearmen, marching towards the chariots on the hill. Behind them, archers made ready, while Addad's horsemen rode out to cover the flanks. Nintinugga was about to signal the attack when a boulder came flying over the city wall and crashed down on the spearmen. Seconds later, a second and a third followed, cutting a swathe through their advancing ranks. Hofileshgu had finally succeeded in reloading Nineveh's defensive machines for a second strike against the attackers.

"Now or never!" Nintinugga shouted, signalling the attack. "For Marduk and Ishtar!" Sanherib urged the horses forward with his whip, and the chariots of Mari thundered down the hill like a tidal wave. The officers among the spearmen were still trying to restore order when the chariots mowed them down. The Mari fighters drove their chariots straight through Addad's troops, splitting them in two. Shouts, cracking timbers, and the ring of iron on iron mingled with the neighs of horses and the rumble of the chariots. Addad's archers tried desperately to pick targets among the chariots that ploughed through their ranks and turned just before they reached the city walls.

From the tower above the city gate, Sargon saw the tide turning in their favour. Now it was time to support the chariots. "Ezira!" he called to his general. "You and Senezon take your units and advance up the centre. Tell the chariots to take the flanks." Ezira acknowledged the order with a wave. The makeshift gate swung open, and the troops moved out. Sanherib saw the movement at the city gate and steered his chariot towards the šagana leading Nineveh's troops.

Ezira, recognising them immediately, beamed to see the gal-ug and Nintinugga again. "Cover our flanks while we push through the middle!" he shouted to them. "We have only nine units left. Most of all, keep the riders off our backs." Nintinugga nodded even as

Sanherib turned away to pass the orders to the other charioteers.

But a new danger was now approaching from the river. The muskil had returned. Dust swirled as they galloped through the ruins of the riverside huts. Their leader had realised that Nineveh's archers had withdrawn from the southern walls, and deduced correctly that they were going to aid the troops in the north. Moving after them, the muskil arrived too late to stop the chariot charge on Addad's ground troops. But they quickly regrouped to lead the remaining units from the river side against Nineveh's defenders and the new arrivals. The mere presence of the muskil reinvigorated Addad's fighters. With renewed determination, they threw themselves into the battle—and Nineveh's troops fought back just as valiantly. The muskil concentrated their fire on the chariots, once again demonstrating their legendary mastery of the bow. Each arrow found its mark as they picked off the charioteers, the horses trampling on out of control into their own ranks.

Sanherib, holding his chariot a little apart to keep an overview, had to reorient. Then he became aware of movement on the road from the north, where a cloud of dust rose, kicked up by many boots approaching in step. Fresh troops were advancing on Nineveh. Sanherib steered his chariot in the direction of the newcomers. When he drew near, he recognised a familiar coat of arms on their standards: the eagle's head of the city of Nemrik. He raised the banner of Ishtar and galloped towards the grouped officers riding ahead of their troops—the governor was personally leading her gal-ugs. She recognised Sanherib driving the Akkadian chariot.

He saluted: "Nadot-kil, ruler of Nemrik! Thank Ish-tar! You are just in time. Nineveh and our queen are in great danger."

She returned his greeting. "So this is how her fears have been realised. Ride with me and tell me what is happening as we advance." Then to her troops she called, "Brave women and men of Nemrik, this is your day. Show Addad what it means to challenge our god-dess Ishtar. For Nineveh!"

She shouted the last words after her soldiers, who were already charging at Addad's fighters, now beset by infantry and chariots from several sides, while archers fired flaming arrows at them from the city walls, adding to the chaos. Countless muskil fell, too. Addad's leader realised how hopeless their situation was and signalled the retreat. Nemrik's foot soldiers pursued the fleeing enemy, who continued to come under fire from the walls. Finally, few who had tried to take Nineveh for Addad left the battlefield alive. Marduk's rising sun il-luminated a battlefield littered with corpses. Nineveh, with the help of their newfound brothers in arms, had survived.

While doctors tended to the injured, Sargon sought out his officers. Senezon, although covered in blood from head to toe, had only suffered a minor scrape or two. Ever-prudent Ezira, too, was unharmed, and Nin-tinugga had also come through unscathed. The king quietly noticed the looks the young woman exchanged with her Subartuan charioteer and guessed that her life had found a new centre. He wondered at himself at the pain of farewell he felt rising within him. But that pain was eclipsed immediately by a greater one when Gusur's body was brought to him. A bull's horn had passed through the boy's chest and into his heart. The king's knees failed him at the sight, and tears filled his eyes. He did not hear the sound of hooves as Urta and her Anat-worshipping hunters appeared. They knelt before the man who had come to them as a stranger and left this earth as their friend. Finally it fell to Ezira to help his king back to his feet.

The prince's body was lifted onto a chariot and carried into the city for which he had given his life.

Twenty-First Chapter:
The Farewell

In the great hall of Nineveh, Queen Semiramis was
holding council. She had been unable to rest since the
attack. Her head ached from attending to all the re-
quests being put to her.

Governor Samše kept a little apart. After the failed
defence of the merchants' new dock, she had suffered
the weight of serious reproach. Woranola had reported
to the queen that the governor had ignored the chain
of command during the battle, and Semiramis had relieved the governor of her duties until the matter was
fully clarified. A tribunal would determine her future.

When the most urgent tasks had finally been dealt
with, Semiramis could devote herself to the delega-
tion from Nemrik. "Thank you, Nadot-kil, for taking it
upon yourself to lead the troops to Nineveh," she said.
"Your arrival turned the tide and gave us victory." The
woman bowed gratefully. "But I wonder," the queen
continued, "why you arrived so late? My messenger
should have alerted you two weeks ago."

"Your messenger never reached Nemrik, Your Majesty. Her body was found under stones near a village to
the north of here." She handed Semiramis the chain
with the amulet of Ishtar and said, "A shepherd's dog
drew its master's attention to the place where her body

was hidden. She had an arrow in her back, and in her pockets he found your clay tablet. We left as soon as we received the news."

Semiramis was stunned. An outrage! *Who would kill an emissary of Ishtar?* she asked herself.

"We don't think she was killed by bandits," Nadot-kil went on, and she held up a leather pouch. "She still had this on her, too."

Semiramis looked towards the governor, who was conspicuously silent. Samše held her gaze and did not flinch. *Are you behind this?* the queen thought with dismay. *Are you actually capable of murdering your own citizens?*

The governor seemed to read her thoughts. "Bands of robbers have always made the road to Nemrik dangerous," she said. "No doubt Addad guessed that Nineveh would call for help and sent out his spies. It was a mistake not to provide the messenger with an escort."

Semiramis eyed the governor but said nothing. The woman had something to hide. She could sense it. But that would have to wait. More urgent matters had to be decided.

King Sargon stood wordlessly beside the throne, gazing into space. He no longer took any part in Nineveh's affairs. Semiramis knew he would rather be alone with his grief, but now was not the time. They had an important decision to make. And he was not there by himself. The officers who had led the battle for Nineveh were also present. Nintinugga and Sanherib stood a little apart, as if not wanting to draw the attention of the others.

Semiramis addressed them all. "Our scouts have confirmed that the battle is over. Addad's soldiers have either fallen or fled into the desert. Many of the muskil have also lost their lives, although we did not kill them all. Addad has no army left to terrorise the people."

"And none left to defend himself, either" Senezon added grimly. "We have a score to settle with him. He should pay for this attack."

"Do you want to go on fighting, Senezon?" asked Semiramis, although she knew his answer. "Haven't enough people died already?"

Senezon shook his axe vigorously. "People, yes. But the evil is still there. If we don't follow through now, Addad will rise again. He must be put out of action once and for all."

Semiramis turned to Sargon, standing beside her. "King Sargon . . . what do you think?" she asked tentatively.

His mind seemed to be far away, but he growled between clenched teeth, "Make him pay! He has mocked the gods far too long. Now is our time to pay him back!"

Revenge, thought Semiramis. *Is that what you want? Revenge will not bring your son back to life. We've accomplished so much, Sargon. Do you want to risk it all for the sake of vengeance?* She turned to the governor who had come to Nineveh's aid at last. "What do you say, Nadot-kil?"

Still heated from the victory outside the walls, Nadot-kil said, "Your Majesty, let us attack! We will show Addad what it means to challenge Ishtar and her people. He will fall."

"Hofileshgu? Your counsel?" The queen now turned her attention to the most experienced of Nineveh's officers.

She also nodded her agreement. "Your Majesty, thank you for asking me. It is time. We can take the war to his realm and put an end to the evil there. I also favour an attack."

"Sanherib?" the queen asked the young man who had been her faithful aide for so many years and who now stood at another woman's side. Seeing the two of them together, Semiramis, like Sargon, felt the pain of parting.

"Decide and I will follow, Majesty," Sanherib said. "My opinion is not important."

"Important or not, I want to hear it," she persisted.

Without hesitation, he replied, "Šagana Senezon is right. We must attack Addad, and we must do it now."

Semiramis's eyes shifted thoughtfully from her confidant to the young woman at his side. *You too, Sanherib,* she thought sadly. *You have only just begun to know love. Do you want to risk that happiness again so quickly?*

She let her gaze wander around the group. Almost all of them wanted to counterattack, despite how unknowable the outcome would be. Only Governor Samše said nothing. Had they forgotten that Addad was of divine origin? The mountains were his realm. He had never been challenged there. Were they so certain he had no troops left and was not already preparing to ambush them?

As Semiramis vacillated, Sargon spoke emphatically. "Addad will not forget this day, Semiramis. If you want to root out the danger to your people once and for all, it must be now."

She looked at him and thought, *And what will happen to our peoples when their common enemy is defeated? Will they turn against each other again?*

He seemed to guess her thoughts. "Many in Nineveh have seen what our people can achieve if we stand together. And one day, when they are asked how Addad was defeated, they will pass it on to their children. If we stop the fight now, we deliver them to his vengeance."

"Never leave a defeated enemy resentful!" Senezon snarled. "Let us finish it!" He punctuated his words with a threatening swing of his axe. The others followed his example.

Semiramis capitulated. "So be it! Let it be known to all that the combined forces of Akkad and Subartu are moving against Addad. But first, let us say our farewells to those who have laid down their lives for us." *One in particular*, she added silently, looking at Sargon.

High above Nineveh, the white temple of Ishtar was crowned the mighty stepped pyramid. Every night, hundreds of worshippers climbed the steep stairs to the altar of the goddess, before which they prayed for help, offered sacrifices, or sought advice from the priesthood. But that night, the ziggurat was deathly quiet.

Samše made her way from the palace to the temple accompanied by three men, the last loyal members of her once glorious guard. The others had all died in the battle. *I have nothing left*, the governor thought bitterly. Nineveh's troops were now under the unconditional command of the Akkadians, the merchants had suffered immense losses and were already looking to Akkad to revive their trade, and the city council had had to admit before Queen Semiramis that it had underestimated the danger Addad posed. She could no longer expect any support from them. It was only a matter of time before she would be asked to resign . . . or worse. But Samše had never been a woman to sit by idly and wait. She had always taken her fate into her own hands, and the gods had been merciful to her. And she was sure they would approve her decision today, too.

A single guard stood at the foot of the steep stairs that led up to the temple. Nineveh had successfully repelled the attackers, and the temple was in no danger that night, so the guard stood alone. The man had raised his spear, but immediately lowered it again when he recognised the city guard.

"You are on the alert, Su-kun," Samše praised the young man, who bowed dutifully to her." Ishtar and Queen Semiramis will be happy to know you are watching over the temple."

"I am only doing my duty, Ma'am," he replied sheepishly. "It is nothing of note."

The governor nodded. "I would like to see for my-self that everything is ready for the funeral," she said. "Is the other guard still up at the sanctuary?"

The man shook his head.

"She has been discharged. King Sargon wishes to spend the night alone with his son. Our job is to secure the entrances to the temple, no more."

Samše raised an eyebrow. "A high honour indeed, to entrust the temple of Ishtar to the Akkadian. But I suppose he deserves it." The man did not dare to reply, and she continued, "I would like to go up and offer my condolences."

"I am sorry, governor," Su-kun said. "I am afraid you will have to wait. The queen's instructions were clear."

Samše glanced at one of her companions and gave him an almost imperceptible wink. The man under-stood and approached the guard from the side. Two more steps. The governor only had to keep him dis-tracted.

"Can you tell me where we will be holding the cere-mony tomorrow?"

The sentry turned towards the temple to point out the site, turning his back on Samše's guard. With one step the man was on him. He thrust his sword into Su-kun's back while he stifled his scream with his other hand. The guard collapsed.

Samše was satisfied. "Quickly! Sargon is alone with his son's body in the temple. If we are quick, we can end the Akkadian royal line and maybe still prevent this senseless attack on Addad."

To avoid attention, she left one of her guards to take Su-kun's place. Then they hid his body and climbed the stairs.

The citizens of Nineveh had laid Prince Gusur out on a wooden frame and set it up in front of the altar of the goddess Ishtar. His body had been washed, his wounds bandaged, and they had clothed him in precious fabrics. On his right they had laid his sword and on his left the hunters from the hills had added a horse's bridle.

Sargon knelt before the wooden frame on which his son's body lay. Along with his loneliness, a dreadful grief was spreading inside him. Senseless . . . how senseless everything had become. The battle for Nineveh, the alliance with Semiramis, his entire reign. What was the point of any of it?

Tears found their way through his clenched eyelids and down his dusty cheeks until they soaked the king's beard, just as the blood of the fallen had soaked the soil outside the gates of Nineveh. Sargon wanted no one around him that night. He wanted to be alone with his memories, recalling so many moments with Gusur. He remembered the little creature they had brought him the day he was born, and how the boy had grown up skilled and strong. He remembered the day when Gusur had sat alone on the back of a horse for the first time. His mother had wailed in fear for her son, but the boy sat securely in the saddle from the very first moment and looked at his parents as if to say, "Don't worry about me! This is my world. Nothing will ever happen to me up here." And he was right. As long as he was in the saddle, no harm could befall him. But on the ground . . .

Another heavy tear streamed down Sargon's cheek. His fist clenched the pommel of his sword, still caked with blood from the fighting. Dust and grime still clung to his clothes. His hair was as tangled as his thoughts, and in his large palms his tears mixed with the desert sand to form a salty grit that scraped his cheeks roughly as he buried his face in his hands. A sorrow immeasurably deep filled the large hall over which Ishtar's eyes watched.

From the high entrance to the sanctuary, Samše studied the kneeling king and cautiously examined the room. Sargon was alone, unprotected. She nodded to her companions, who silently drew their swords and crept on tiptoe into the temple. Sargon was still deep in his memories of his son and oblivious to everything around him. Samše's men crept forward silently until one of them came to a halt directly behind the king. He glanced back questioningly at his mistress. She nodded. The guard raised his sword to deliver the killing stroke, but there it stopped, suspended in mid-air. An arrow jutted from the man's chest. He gasped and dropped his weapon, which clattered to the floor.

The sound jolted Sargon out of his thoughts and he turned to see his would-be assassin twitching on the temple floor. Behind him, he saw another man with a drawn sword. Suddenly, his grief was forgotten. Unbridled rage rose inside him. He unsheathed his sword grimly. "Haven't had enough killing, have you?" he snapped at the stranger. "Is that all you know how to do? Sneak up and stab a man in the back?" The king strode towards him, and he backed away uncertainly. He'd been told to expect a grief-stricken old man crippled by mourning. But now he was facing a fighter.

Sargon swung his sword menacingly. He'd had enough of it all, enough of Nineveh's honeyed talk and intrigues, enough of the feigned civility and political plots that had ensnared all of them and viciously, underhandedly killed his son. And here stood one of the murderers. *You or me*, Sargon thought dourly. *One of us will not leave this room alive.*

With a mighty blow, he swung at the assassin. The man parried the swing and took another step back towards the entrance. "Fight back, coward!" Sargon bawled. "Fight or I'll slash your belly wide open." He swung at the man again, who was only able fend off the mighty blow with difficulty. Then he stabbed back at the king. Sargon was pleased to see that the man was ready to fight. He deflected the man's thrust easily and swung again. The clang of metal on metal rang through the temple portico. In the light of the torches, the fighters' shadows flickered like dark giants across the walls. Sargon drove his victim ruthlessly across the room. He fought as if in a frenzy. In his mind's eye, he saw once again how they had beaten his son in that same room. The images rushed before his eyes: Samše's accusations against Gusur, who had found allies to help the city, allies that Samše refused to even look for. Back then, Sargon had drawn his sword against her, but had sheathed it again. Tonight he would not make the same mistake.

The assassin had recovered from his initial shock. His strikes were now stronger, his movements more coordinated. Sargon was facing a worthy opponent. The man lacked the king's fighting experience, but he had enough strength in his arms to parry his blows. Sargon took a step back before his next assault, and the opponents circled each other warily. Then a whistling sound whirred through the room, followed by a muffled thud. A black-feathered arrow jutted from the assassin's chest. He collapsed where he stood. Sargon wheeled around as Nintinugga emerged from behind a pillar.

"You were too close to him, sire. I couldn't risk hitting you," she apologised dryly.

She went across to him, her eyes scanning the hall, and she saw a figure dart out through the entrance. *Two dead, one on the run*, Nintinugga thought with satisfaction. She fell to her knees before her king.

"My king, please forgive me for doing my duty unbidden. It was simply too dangerous to leave you alone in this city."

"You should have asked permission," he chided her, but he was not harsh.

"Ezira gave me his blessing," the young woman defended herself. "Even Sanherib thought it was reckless of you to come to the temple alone."

"It's all right," Sargon replied. Slowly, the king of Akkad was returning to reality. He looked at the motionless figures of the men who'd come to kill him. It was over. His rage had evaporated. Clear thoughts flowed into his mind like the gentle breeze that wafted from the temple gates to where they stood in the hall.

"There are only two lying here. I could have sworn there were three."
Nintinugga nodded. "The third has run. He can't be far yet."

"Then go and get him," Sargon ordered. "But keep him alive. I want to know who's behind this." Nintinugga turned and darted out of the temple.

Samše rushed down the steps. From above she could see her last companion, the guard she had left at the foot of the ziggurat.

"En-kan!" she called from above. "Take me to the stables, now! I have to leave Nineveh at once."

"En-kan won't be carrying out any orders of yours anymore," the man from below replied, turning around. "And you will not be leaving Nineveh."

Samše stopped as if she had run into an invisible wall. It was Sanherib, gal-ug of Semiramis's guard.

"Please do not resist," Sanherib said. "Your guard did a good job of disguising himself. Unfortunately, he seemed to forget that palace guards carry spears, not swords." He gestured up to her. "Come down, please. Queen Semiramis would like to ask you some questions."

Samše had quickly regained her composure. "Gal-ug Sanherib, as a faithful servant of Subartu, it is your duty to protect me from the Akkadians." She descended with measured steps. As she drew nearer, she slid her right hand slowly behind her back, where she carried a dagger in her belt. Samše was not a particularly athletic woman. She would have little chance in a duel with the powerfully built gal-ug. But the dagger was coated with a viper's poison. The tinies cut would be fatal.

Sanherib let her draw closer. "You are mistaken. It is the Akkadians who are protecting us from Addad. We owe them our gratitude."

Samše had almost reached him. Sanherib, apparently unaware of the danger, had his right hand outstretched to help her down the last steps, his bare arm unpro-

tected by armour. Samše silently unsheathed her dagger. Then a whistling sounded, growing rapidly louder
before suddenly coming to a stop. The arrow struck
Samše cleanly in the back, pierced her heart, and exit-
ed through her chest. The governor slumped onto the
steps.

"Hasn't anyone ever told you that you're far too
trusting?" Nintinugga's angry voice snapped from
above. She was standing on the top step of the temple
with her bow still raised. Then Sanherib saw the dagger
in the dead woman's hand. He swallowed.

"Queen Semiramis did once mention something like
that."

"Then you should have listened to her. You said
yourself that she was a very smart woman."

He did not reply but climbed the steps and took Nintinugga in his arms.

The following night, Sargon ascended again to the
sanctuary of Ishtar. He was followed by Senezon,
Ezira, Nintinugga, and the gal-ugs of Nineveh. Flags
bearing the coats of arms of Subartu and Akkad had
been raised on the first platform, where the combined
forces of Nineveh and Nemrik had assembled. The
beating of drums filled the night and accompanied the
mourners' steps, the only sound to be heard in Nineveh
on that windless night.

Servants of the temple stood with torches along the
steps from the first platform to the uppermost level,
where the temple stood that had so magically, so per-
ilously, attracted Gusur that night. This time, the sanctuary was filled with mourners there to pay their last
respects to the prince.

Sargon strode up the pale tiled steps. The white temple glowed in the bright moonlight. Addad no longer had the power to hide the city from Ishtar's sight, and stars twinkled above the white walls of Nineveh's highest sanctum. The temple gates were wide open and radiant light shone out at the king and his retinue. To the left of the temple, the hunters who had come to mean so much to Gusur stood in a single line. They were carrying the flag of Anat, as they had always done when Gusur had held the races in honour of the goddess. He had become one of them.

Opposite the hunters, a funeral pyre had been erected. Gusur was seated on a scaffold of the finest cedar wood, positioned so that he could depart the world as if he were astride a horse. His face was turned towards the mountains to the east, where he had first encountered the hunters and where the sun would soon rise. The sound of lutes and rattles announced the approach of Ishtar's priests, who now emerged from the temple. The high priestess led the procession, with Semiramis walking at her side. The queen wore her long white dress and the headband with the symbol of Ishtar. Her face shone brighter than ever. She carried a silken shawl draped over one arm, which she would offer as a burial gift for the dead. The holy dignitaries followed in their long robes, each swinging a small brazier containing incense and precious herbs.

The procession moved around the pyre until it came to a halt on the side facing the moon. The drums fell silent as the horns of Anat's hunters softly rose in a lament for the deceased warrior. The sound carried far across the city to the hills that Gusur had so often explored with them. Sargon felt himself lifted and carried by the song and reminded of the many experiences he had shared with his son, of his eager smile, his unquestioning loyalty, his sense of duty. Gusur had followed his father wherever he went and was known for standing by those who confided in him.

The song of the horns grew louder. Sargon looked out over the rooftops of the city to the east, where Marduk's sun was already heralding its rise. Semiramis was standing beside the king and gazing in the same direction. *Ishtar is kind*, she thought. *She is leaving this moment to Marduk.* And indeed, the moon of her goddess sank from view as the first rays of the sun made the distant mountain peaks glow. The sun god appeared over the land so used to fearing him. This time, however, Marduk came not as a conqueror, but to receive one of his own. More and more, his radiance filled the sky above the city. The horns grew louder still, and the drums again began to play. Then the first rays touched the gables of the temple of Ishtar, illuminating them in glittering gold.

Semiramis looked on as the sanctuary of Ishtar, so high above the city, glowed in Marduk's warm colours. The morning light inched further and further down the walls until it found the funeral pyre. Then, at last, the glowing ball of the sun appeared fully behind the mountains. The horns and drums drowned out every other sound.

Sargon looked at the torch he carried in his left hand. It was time to say farewell. He took a step forward, but it was difficult. His whole body seemed to resist letting his son go to the realm of the dead. But he forced himself to keep going. Senezon, Ezira, and Nintinugga followed him in silence. The king continued to move forward, his every fibre tense. Then the rays of his god's sun touched him, too, and gave him new strength. He felt the warm rays travel from his head to his shoulders to his chest. Marduk was ready to receive the dead man. Two steps away, he lifted the torch and plunged it deep into the pyre, which caught fire instantly. Then he retreated a few steps to stay clear of the flames. Not a breath of wind disturbed the fire. Its smoke rose skyward in a seemingly endless column, visible even in distant regions—and the people knew that today a great one had passed. The fire burned for a long time while Marduk's sun rose over the city. And when the fire finally burned out, the sun stood high above the temple square to absorb the last wisps of smoke. All that remained was a heap of ashes beside a king upon whom a foreign land gazed.

The evening after the funeral, the high priestess went to see the queen. She found her with King Sargon, surrounded by countless clay tablets and studying a map. The map showed the mountains north of the city, where they suspected Addad's fortress to be. The priestess bowed.

"Queen Semiramis, King Sargon, I am grateful to you for entrusting me with the funeral. I hope you were pleased with the outcome." The whole city was talking about the spectacle of how Ishtar and Marduk had come together to farewell the dead prince on his final journey. Never before had the once hostile deities been part of a ceremony together. The temple of Nineveh had been the stage for a great spectacle that would be talked about a hundred years from now.

It was Sargon who replied. "I am indebted to you, High Priestess," he said. "Gusur would certainly never have thought it possible for you to do him such an honour." He avoided any mention of his son's first night at the temple.

She thanked him for his words and turned to the queen. "Your Majesty, the temple servants wish to erect a stele to commemorate the ceremony where the deceased was laid to rest. Would you agree to this?" she asked. "The temple will bear the cost, of course," she added quickly.

Semiramis considered her offer. Reports of the ceremony and how the smoke had risen towards the sun had spread throughout the city. Merchants were already spreading word of the miracle in Nineveh, where an Akkadian prince was welcomed by both Ishtar and Marduk. The number of pilgrims visiting Ishtar's temple would only increase. *And with them the temple's income,* the queen concluded. The priestess's suggestion was not entirely altruistic.

"Thank you for your generous offer," Semiramis said. "I too would welcome the erection of a stele to commemorate the defender of Nineveh where our citizens will remember him." She looked to Sargon, who nodded his agreement. "However," the queen continued, "I would like to see it in a different location. Prince Gusur never felt at home up at the temple." She avoided noting that he had also been sentenced to death there. "But he would certainly appreciate being able to attend our equestrian competitions in the future. Build the stele at the racetrack in the north. I hereby entrust you also with overseeing the building of a new sanctuary out there. To Anat."

That had certainly taken the high priestess by surprise. Sargon smiled. The costs for the stele and the new sanctuary would be far higher than what the priestess had in mind, but the temple of Ishtar was rich. Gusur had always felt far more connected to the races held in Anat's name than to the temple of Ishtar, however magnificent it might be.

It took her a moment, but the high priestess finally overcame her surprise. She agreed happily. Inwardly, she was probably already calculating how many pilgrims the new holy site would attract. Semiramis guessed the priestess's thoughts and smiled to herself. Senezon talked often about how everyone in Nineveh thought like a shopkeeper. *And he is not wrong,* the queen thought.

Then the high priestess noticed the leather pouch on the queen's table. "Was that the one found with the messenger?" she asked.

Semiramis frowned. Did the high priestess know something about it?

"It is," she confirmed. "We are still puzzling over who carried out the attack."

The high priestess took a deep breath, then said, "They were men from Nineveh."

Semiramis was struck silent for a moment. Sargon stood up and took a step towards the high priestess. He looked her in the eye, but the woman could not meet his glare.

Semiramis came to her aid. In a gentle, encouraging voice she said, "Speak, priestess. What can you tell us?"

The woman fell to her knees before the throne, as Ishtar's image gazed sternly down on her. Her voice trembled as she spoke. "A man from our governor's guard gave his girl some silver coins. He told her he received it for stopping an important messenger. He was supposed to stop the message from being delivered, no more, but they were only able to stop the messenger with an arrow." She avoided looking her queen in the eye. "The man was bragging to the girl. He was showing off, telling her how the governor had entrusted him with such an important mission. Then the girl told me."

Semiramis listened to the priestess's explanation. Her face was a mask of stone as she tried to contain her anger at the betrayal.

"Where is the man now?" she asked.

"He died at the docks," the priestess replied. "Ishtar has judged him."

"And how will our goddess judge you for concealing this treachery from your queen?"

"Your Majesty, please forgive me!" the woman wailed, pressing her face to the floor in front of the queen. "I didn't know what to think anymore. Addad had never shown any hostility towards our city. Our governor even had plans to build a temple to him. And the Akkadians had been at war with us for years. We lost so many young men and women on the front lines at Assur. Were we to suddenly believe that they did not want to take Nineveh for themselves? Their god did so much harm to Ishtar. We thought we had to protect you from him and his monsters."

"His 'monsters,' as you call them, were born of your own imagination, no more. It was you who called them that when they inadvertently broke our rules." She had not forgotten the high priestess's inflated accusations against Gusur.

"I want to make it up to you," the woman said, desperately looking up at Semiramis. "Your Majesty, you were right about Addad. And we should have treated the Akkadians better. And it was not right to condemn Prince Gusur so hastily or to ban the Akkadians from the city. All we did was hand them over to Addad's forces. Please, let me prove it."

Semiramis hesitated. She looked up at the statue of her goddess and saw how the fingers of Ishtar's raised right hand were not closed to strike, but open, as if to bless the beholder. Yes, Ishtar was the goddess of war, but she was also the goddess of love.

The high priestess pointed to the map and the clay tablets. "Queen Semiramis, King Sargon, it is true what they say, isn't it?" she asked. "You are planning to continue the fight against Addad." It was more a statement than a question.

Sargon sighed. "Now would be the right moment for it. His forces have been crushed. A few of the muskil escaped, but the thunder god should have little support otherwise."

"But he is not completely defenceless," Semiramis added. "From here to his fortress is probably six days' journey. We don't have enough wagons to supply our troops for a journey that long. We can send for more from Nemrik and Nimrud, but that will take weeks."

The high priestess had an idea.

"Your Majesty, as representative of the temple, let me take care of providing for your troops. If you wish, they will be able to leave the day after tomorrow."

Semiramis was taken aback. What did the woman have in mind? The priestess looked complacently at the confusion on the faces of the two royals. Then she explained her plan. Sargon brightened. For the first time since the Akkadians had been forced out of Nineveh, his loud laughter rang through the palace. Addad's days were numbered.

Senezon personally supervised the loading of the wagons that were to supply his troops on their way to Addad's mountain fortress. He hated finding out that important supplies were missing when he was already underway. This time, however, his fears were unfounded. Even barrels of beer had been provided for the troops.

"The traders here have more wagons than Nineveh has soldiers," he said as he paced the staging area with Ezira and Woranola. "I'm starting to think that Nineveh's filled with nothing but hucksters."

"What do you mean 'starting'?" his old friend asked. "You've been saying that ever since we got here." The spearman looked at the loaded wagons already waiting at the gate. "I rather wonder what that high priestess promised them to get them to give up their wagons. They're practically falling over themselves with offers."

"I can help you there," Senezon said with a broad grin. "Queen Semiramis whispered the story in my ear. According to her, every now and then our helpers here like to partake in the festivities with the virgins in the temple. The high priestess announced yesterday that anyone refusing to support the campaign against Add-ad will not be welcome at the temple ever again."

"Men!" sneered Woranola, walking with them through the rows of wagons. "All you ever think with is what's between your legs. Why is that?"

"Someone jealous?" Senezon laughed and gave her a good-natured pat on the shoulder. The archer shrugged his hand away but smiled.

The force that set out from Nineveh to destroy once and for all the power of the thunder god made slow progress. Urta led her hunters ahead as scouts. They were followed by the king and queen and their officers. Behind them came the main force, led by the troops from Nemrik under the command of governor Nad-ot-kil, and two heavy transport wagons, each holding one of the catapults. The Akkadian and Subartuan foot soldiers brought up the rear, some armed with spears, others with bows. Subartu had not seen such a large army on the march since the great wars. But Semiramis was not fooled by the imposing sight. The fresh memory of their joint victory was the glue keeping the soldiers together. *But new memories fade quickly. Old enmities live much longer,* the queen thought. Addad would only have to stall the troops long enough, and the old rivals would turn on each other again.

They travelled by night, according to the custom in Subartu. The roads around Nineveh were wide and easily passable, and even the charioteers from Mari could guide their chariots safely through the darkness. But the further they got from the city, the rougher the road became. From the third day on, it was little more than a dusty dirt track, with stelae here and there indicating that were on the route to the mountains.

Twenty-Second Chapter:
Old Secrets

It was quiet in the camp when Semiramis began her rounds. Soldiers on the march sometimes developed quirks or traits that they would never adopt in peacetime. The queen had therefore made it her habit, early in her reign, to inspect her troops personally when they stopped to rest. She found nothing out of the ordinary, except that Akkad's once despised chariots were now being guarded alongside the oxcarts from Subartu as if it were a matter of course. Some soldiers were sleeping in their tents, while others huddled around fires, cooking, telling stories about their daring deeds, real and imagined. *At least the soldiers from Akkad and Subartu brag the same way,* Semiramis thought, and a smile flickered on her face. The further behind them the attack on Nineveh was, the greater the courage became. It felt good to not have any other worries that day.

Five nights had passed since their departure. The road into the mountains was climbing steadily. So far there was no sign of Addad or his followers. The thunder god seemed to have withdrawn all his remaining forces to the mountains. Semiramis had expected this. In the narrow gorges, where the chariots would be useless, resistance would be all the more effective. Until that point, the queen left her troops to enjoy their tales of past exploits.

On the way back to her tent, she caught sight of Nintinugga. She was with Sanherib a short way outside the camp. They were practising with her bow. Then Semiramis recalled something strange she had noticed about the archer during the battle—now would be the time to clarify it. She moved closer, staying behind a rock from where she could observe them unseen. And there it was: the young woman from Akkad was not using her own bow, but Sanherib's. *They must have become very close indeed on their journey,* the queen thought, *if the boy is letting her use that masterpiece.* With an expert eye, she assessed Nintinugga's shooting. *Outstanding,* she had to admit. The young woman had clearly learned archery from an early age. And she had the requisite respect for the splendid weapon. But did she really understand the treasure she held in her hand?

Nintinugga had set up her target ten paces further away than the archers before her. Sanherib's bow never ceased to amaze her. Its accuracy seemed independent of the distance to the target—a small disc, barely visible now, but she did not doubt she would hit it again.

Sanherib sat a little apart, lost in thought, watching her arrows whir through the air. Nintinugga was too focussed on her training to notice the queen approaching from behind and she jumped when the woman in her many-layered dress appeared beside her.

"You draw too slowly, Nintinugga," said the queen, moving over the stony ground as silently as ever. "Kalbaba's bow requires an archer who is sure of herself."

Sanherib had jumped to his feet at the sound of the queen's voice. He bowed deeply, a little conscience-stricken that his inattention allowed her to sneak up on them.

Nintinugga carefully lifted the arrow from the string and looked at the queen. Semiramis saw suspicion and curiosity in her eyes. "Do you know the bow, Your Majesty?" the young woman asked.

Semiramis replied with the merest of nods. "That is Ulan-Nun, the Infallible. It was completed on a full moon night just before Sanherib was born," she said softly, as if speaking to herself. Her gal-ug looked at her in confusion. He had told no one but Nintinugga about the bow.

Semiramis smiled at him. "I recognised the bow when you first entered my service. It was wise of you to practise with it only covertly. What better way to keep your mother's secret?" Then she turned to Nintinugga and, a little louder and in a stern, teacherly voice, said, "Now show us whether you are really equal to Ulan-Nun! No more wavering, no more weighing things when you start to draw." The queen stood and faced Nintinugga, just outside her firing line. "You can see the target. Now learn to feel it too. Picture the arrow entering the target in the middle. And then take an arrow and do not hesitate!"

Nintinugga looked first at the queen, then towards her distant target.

"Do not think about your draw!" the queen continued. "Think only of what you are shooting at." Nintinugga's focus shifted into the distance. Then she nocked an arrow onto the string and drew it back powerfully. At the same time her left arm raised the bow to the level of the target. Her arm reached the right shooting height just as the string was at its limit, and she let the arrow fly. She closed her eyes and listened to it. A muffled thud in the distance signalled a hit. Nintinugga opened her eyes again. The arrow was in the target—two fingers off centre, as she would see later. But Semiramis did not look satisfied.

"You think too long about your shot, Nintinugga. You worry when your target is small or far away. You don't see how you are fighting the bow. Let it go! Let it do its job! Concentrate on your target, nothing else. Ulan-Nun knows how to get there."

Nintinugga hesitated. She was already the best of the Akkadian archers and Sanherib's bow had only underlined her mastery. But she also knew that something was missing, and Semiramis seemed to know about the bow. Nintinugga knew she could not rest until she knew everything about it, too.

"I'm ready," she said plainly.

"I will tell you your target, Nintinugga," the queen said. "There will be many of them and I will give you time to picture each one in your mind. And then shoot! Forget everything else! Focus your mind only on your target, never on your aim!"

Nintinugga let herself be guided by the queen's words. She chose a place where her footing was firm. Ulan-Nun swung as if weightless in her hand, following every movement of her arm. Nintinugga loved how obedient the bow felt—and she felt as if she could rely on it always. But today there was something else. The bow seemed lighter, almost excited, like a racehorse skittish with anticipation before a race. *Does the bow suspect what's coming?*

"Do not be surprised. You will shoot your arrows in quicker succession than ever before, Nintinugga," Semiramis said "Trust the bow to find its way. Relax and let go!" Nintinugga almost recoiled at the queen's last words. Uncertain, she looked over at Sanherib. He hesitated a moment, but then nodded encouragingly.

Nintinugga set the quiver of arrows down beside her and took the first one that came to hand. Semiramis pointed to the practise target beside Nintinugga's. "There!" Nintinugga turned swiftly towards the target. Her eyes took in the braided fibres with the painted rings. In her mind, she could almost feel the rough stalks between her fingers and smell the cut straw.

Instantly, tension built in her body. The arrow was already flying from the string, and Semiramis was already pointing to her next target.

When the queen paused, just moments later, Nintinugga had loosed twenty-four arrows. Each had found its target, be it one of the practice boards, a hanging branch, even a bird flying by. The bow truly was infallible. Nintinugga realised her heart was racing. She was drenched in sweat. Sanherib had watched the spectacle with unbelieving eyes. Semiramis simply smiled.

"Treat your bow like you would a man, Nintinugga," the queen said. "It is strong-willed but will bend to its limit when the right woman holds it and shows it its target. A wise woman, likewise, knows how to bend a man to her will without breaking him. That's why there are so few men among the real archers."

"How do you know all this?" asked Nintinugga. "Did you know Master Kalbaba?"

"Child, I did not know him. I revered him." The queen stroked the bow as if she had been reunited with a lover after a long time apart. "We women all revered him . . . the master with the perfect hands."

And I almost made him mine, she added silently. Barely sixteen, she had contrived to be alone with the master in his workshop. She had put on her thinnest dress and was looking at him in a way that would have won over any man back then. She was sitting on a stool near his workbench that day and had one bare foot propped on a backrest—a little too high to look innocent, for it made her skirt ride up, revealing her long, slender leg. Kalbaba had moved closer and closer to her as he filed away at a length of wood. Semiramis had felt his eager eyes penetrating the fabric that covered her breasts, and she arched her body to make them stand out even more prominently. She felt herself grow moist at the memory of that evening. His left hand had finally slipped from the wood and was moving towards her leg when a child's cry snapped them both out of their trance. Master Kalbaba tore himself away as if he had woken from a dream, and he returned his concentration to his workpiece.

From that day, he had made sure that she was never alone with him again. *Kal, Kal,* she sighed mentally. *What would have happened if we had made love that night? I would have been yours, and I would have saved you from the assassins.* She hesitated. *Would I really have done that? Or would I have simply followed you to your hut and become as much a victim as you? Ishtar, mistress, your ways are strange, sending me such thoughts again after so many years.*

She realised that Nintinugga was waiting for her to explain. "Sanherib is very much like him. With his broad shoulders, his willingness to accept responsibility. And his patience, his large hands, his loyal heart. People take after their grandparents, they say." She turned her head to the horizon in the west where the sun had just set, as if seeking a memory there.

"I was very young when I first entered the master's workshop," the queen continued. "My mother often bought arrows there, sometimes a bow, if Kalbaba was gracious. He was not a man you could simply order something from. He decided what was made, and for whom. Many princes coveted his bows, but failed to win his favour, and even more women failed in their courtship. He remained faithful to one, Wasanwa. And she gave him four daughters, each more beautiful than the other, and all of them became masters of the bow. He made each of them her own bow, according to her character."

"Sanherib's mother, Hannah, was the eldest. For her, Kalbaba created the Ulan-Nun. It is a bow of the endless steppes, which Hannah loved to explore on horseback. A rider at full gallop has little time to aim, and Ulan-Nun was built for shooting quickly. And yet it still commands the distance, like all the master's bows. Together, Hannah and her sisters watched over the master jealously, as if no other men existed. Only once did she weaken, when she lay with a man at the festival of Ishtar. Ten months later, Sanherib was born, a boy in a house that admitted only daughters."

"Master Kalbaba was furious when he learned she was pregnant, but he was even more furious when his grandson was born. He did not speak a word to Hannah for years, and until the day he died he refused to see his grandson." Now she looked at Sanherib with sad eyes. "Sanherib, you were simply denied. Even your family's closest friends never knew you existed, which is why their killers never sought you out." She saw the pain in Sanherib's eyes. "But your mother was very strong. She built a hut with her own hands, hidden away in the farthest corner of the garden, where she lived with you. Her father forbade either of you from entering the house. But the servants loved you more than anything, especially because you grew up to be the image of your grandfather. In the end, their love is what saved you."

She turned back to Nintinugga. She could see that the woman already knew the family's tragic end.

"A unit of the royal guard found the servants with Sanherib in the desert, half-starved. They brought them to the palace safely while we pursued the prince. One of his lackeys finally revealed his hiding place. We captured him alive and executed him . . . for a whole night his screams pierced the desert while arrows pierced his body. Then the screaming stopped. Master Kalbaba had been avenged, but his family and all his work had burned to ash, all save Sanherib and the bow you now carry." The queen looked at the young woman and added. "Treat it well, Nintinugga. It is the last of its kind."

Sanherib had fallen to his knees. He pressed his face into his hands to hide his tears. "Why are you telling me this now, Majesty? All these years I had no idea you knew my family. Why are you bringing back these memories today?"

The queen felt a tension in her face greater than that in a bow.

"Tomorrow we will face a god, Sanherib. Remember that. No one knows what will happen then. If I die tomorrow, it will be in the knowledge that Kalbaba's grandson has learned his heritage."

With that, she left them and walked back to her tent.

Stones crunched under Sargon's feet as he descended the slope. He had to descend with caution—again and again, loose rocks broke free and rolled ahead of him, as if to announce his arrival in the valley. He had left his bodyguards behind. Should he fall, they would search for him before nightfall and find him here. He was alone, but he did not feel unprotected.

The green of the trees on the slopes was a pleasant contrast to the bare, stony plateaus that crowned the hills. Streams trickled down into the valley, where they joined to form a small river that carried the water to the Tigris. There were no human beings to be seen. Birds circled high in the sky, where Addad had placed individual clouds like sentries, there to announce the arrival of the people. Sargon tightened his grip on the spear he had brought along as a walking stick. He was in Addad's realm. He could be attacked there at any time.

Senezon would be furious if he found out I'd left my guards behind, the king thought. *'You're too reckless, as usual,' he'd say.* But Senezon did not know all the secrets. Sargon felt safe and enjoyed being alone with his thoughts. Nineveh was big and offered many distractions—too many for a man who appreciated the silence of the desert. The rustling of the trees in the wind and the lapping of the water was not silence either, but it was steady and soothing.

Sargon sat down on a large rock that stood above a patch of forest and gazed down into the valley below. A bull was grazing in a meadow, apparently occupied harmlessly with the lush pastures. Sargon, however, was not fooled. He had ruled in the circle of the gods for a very long time. He knew the signs: Addad was watching them. The thunder god had sent his animals to observe their every move. At the right moment, he would strike. Sargon studied the space between himself and the bull. It was about twice as far as he could throw a spear. A stream separated them. Sargon put the spear down at his side. If the bull attacked, he would face it on the bank of the stream, where he would have the higher ground. The bull made no move to approach, but Sargon did not take his eyes off it. *One member of the royal family had already been killed in Subartu by a bull. Gusur . . .*

Tears came to his eyes and trickled down his cheeks at the thought of his son. *Gusur, why did I have to bring you to Subartu?* He had had great plans with his son. Before Gusur ascended to the throne, he was to get to know all the lands his kingdom encompassed. He was to be known by friend and foe alike before he faced them as ruler of Akkad. But it had all been in vain. Now, until a new heir to the throne was found, Sargon once again bore that responsibility. *What would happen if I were to perish on this campaign?* Sargon looked at the bull, but it still showed no interest in him.

Then the king heard a heavy footfall behind him. A strange hissing thrummed in the air. Sargon did not look around. He knew it was no snake.

"Better stay hidden in the trees, old friend," he said aloud, still with his eye on the bull. "Addad's spies are everywhere. He must not see you." A snort told him that he had been heard. Then the ground shook slightly as a mighty body lay down. Like a faithful dog, the serpent-dragon lay close behind Sargon in the undergrowth, and he relaxed. Addad could send a hundred bulls now, but against the mušḫuššu they would have no hope of victory.

When he spoke, he spoke to himself as much as to the serpent-dragon. "Our army is following the road that Addad himself had built. He knows every bend." He pondered for a while. "So far he has not attacked us. But I don't think he will let us get to the gates of his fortress unscathed. Somewhere along the way the attack will come." Again a low hiss came to him. *Does the mušḫuššu really understand me?* he wondered. He and his high priest had tried countless times to summon the mighty beast to help them, but in vain. The mušḫuššu took orders only from its master, and that was Marduk. It followed Marduk just as Sargon did his bidding. *But Marduk understands my words*, Sargon thought. *He will send the mušḫuššu.*

"Stay out of sight. Follow the high ground above us." Sargon continued. "They will attack from above. When that happens, you can strike them from the rear." He cast another suspicious look at the bull, but it did not seem to spy the Akkadian's mighty protector. *And Addad surely has spies within our army, too*, he thought. "Until then, we must keep your presence hidden from the others," he said, resolved. "There will be clefts and caves where you can hide when the trees become too sparse. That is where I will look for you when I need your help."

The bushes at Sargon's back rustled as a large body pushed them aside. Heavy footsteps faded into the forest. Sargon waited another moment. Then he picked up the spear and made his way back to camp.

Twenty-Third Chapter:
The Ascent

They did not start the next stage until well after midnight and kept moving long after the sun had risen. Sargon and Semiramis had agreed to use the daylight from now on—by day they could more easily spot a possible muskil ambush. In the mountains, too, it was no longer so hot, and the Subartuans did not feel as great a need to hide from the sun.

Their path now took them through narrow gorges, the steep sides of which made it impossible for the riders to march in wide formation. The clatter of hooves resounded from the mountain walls. From time to time, large birds sailed overhead, but no other living creature showed itself.

Senezon rode at his king's side. After Gusur's death, he became the king's highest-ranked soldier. Sargon was grateful to have him close. They had saved Nineveh together, but at what cost? The king thought of those who had followed him to Subartu and those who had paid for it with their lives. How many more would die? Addad would surely have noticed their troops by now. Why hadn't he attacked yet? *Because we haven't yet reached the right place,* he thought, answering his own question. The path was narrow and only rarely did a track branch off. It would have been the perfect place for a trap, an ideal spot to waylay an army and destroy it with arrows and stones. But so far the trap had not snapped shut.

Semiramis had described the location of the thunder god's rock fortress to them. On a plateau atop the highest mountain, Addad had built a stepped temple with three platforms. There was only one stairway leading up, and each platform was fortified with walls and towers. Good archers could inflict great losses from above on an attacking force long before they could reach the next platform—and the muskil were fearsome archers. And then there was the thunder god himself. There in the mountains, he was in his element. Some days, the heavy clouds engulfed the temple itself. It was said that Addad could hurl lightning with his bare hands. How presumptuous was it of humans to challenge a god?

Will my life also end here in Subartu? the king wondered more than once on the journey. Turning to Senezon now, he said, "When you return home, I want you to take control of the garrison in Akkad. We can learn a lot from Nineveh's defences."

"When *we* return home, I will never voluntarily set foot in such a cesspool of a city again," Senezon corrected him. His distaste for the thoughtful tone in the king's voice was abundantly clear. "You would have to drag me there in chains."

Sargon smiled at his general's indignation, and his gloomy thoughts evaporated.

"If you're desperate to bring us Subartuan customs, then you'd better send Nintinugga," Senezon continued. "Running a city's for women. That's why Semiramis didn't get any men involved. Nintinugga also knows more about bows and arrows than I ever will, and she seems to have found herself her very own source of Subartuan wisdom. And he doesn't seem too averse to a settled life either." He nodded towards the chariot on which the archer was riding with Sanherib, her arm around his waist.

"Your king has his eye on us," the young man noted.

Nintinugga nodded. "He has since we first arrived in Nineveh."

"Did he say anything to you?"

"He didn't need to. I went to him and told him about everything that had happened since we left the camp."

"Everything? Really?" he asked.

She seemed a little embarrassed by his question, but he liked that. "Well, with some things I didn't go into too much detail. But I told him everything he needed to know."

"What did you tell him about me?"

"That I owe you my life. And that I will never leave your side until the day I die."

He looked at her, puzzled. "Are all Akkadian women from as forthright as you?"

She grinned broadly. "With the right man, all of us." *And not just us Akkadian women,* she mentally added.

There was movement at the head of the column. The hunters were returning, and they had two men in their midst. Sargon ordered a halt and rode forward to the hunters, Semiramis immediately rode to his side. The men wore plain hides and walked barefoot between the riders. They looked at the troops suspiciously—they had never seen so many soldiers before. But they recognised the queen and threw themselves on the ground in front of her horse. Semiramis stopped and dismounted.

"You know me," she said. "Speak! Who are you and where are you from?"

"We are herders from Halal, Your Majesty," said the taller of the two.

"And where is your herd?" the queen asked.

"The muskil stole our goats just as we were getting ready to sleep. Please let us return to our village."

"Where were you grazing your goats?" asked Sargon, who had also dismounted and now approached curiously. The men looked at the king of Akkad in surprise. They did not answer immediately.

"I would like to know that, too," Semiramis reinforced the question.

"A half day's walk from here," the man replied, pointing to a rocky outcrop far behind them. "Below Addad's temple."

"You let your animals graze at the temple of the thunder god?" asked Sargon, puzzled.

The man shrugged. "Why not? The soil is good there. There's plenty of rain. The muskil keep wild animals away from the temple, and until now they'd always left us alone."

"Then how do you know it was them?" asked Semiramis.

"Because we saw them do it," the other man said. "The goats like the grass on the plateau behind the temple. The wind there is usually not so strong. We'd just lain down in a gap in the rocks to sleep when we heard the muskil's hooves. They killed our dogs and herded the goats into the temple."

"Then how did you stay out of sight? The muskil would surely have seen you if you'd passed the temple again to reach the road."

"We found another way, on the east side," the first man explained. "It's steep, but we made it down safely. Their guards didn't see us."

A way to the plateau that the muskil don't know? Sargon thought. This opened up new possibilities. Semiramis seemed to be thinking the same, but she said, "Let us rest now. Give these men something to eat. They must be hungry." Turning to Sargon, she said, "The temple of Addad is very close. Time to gather our officers and plan our attack."

"It's a trap, plain as day," Senezon declared. "Would Addad have overlooked a back way to his fortress all these years? Impossible."

They were sitting close together in a cave that Senezon had discovered near the road. Semiramis and Sargon had made their camp in the back of the cave, dividing the space with a heavy curtain. Now they were all sitting in the front section, while Sanherib and Nintinugga guarded the entrance.

"And yet it holds a lot of promise," Sargon insisted. "No army before us ever marched this deep into the mountains. Addad has never needed to secure his realm any better."

"After Nineveh, I'm sure he has a different opinion on the matter," the broad-shouldered fighter insisted. "I can accept that the muskil stole the herders' goats to bolster their supplies for a siege, but I'll never believe Addad would simply overlook such a gaping hole in his defences."

Semiramis silently followed the Akkadians' heated conversation. She had come to know and appreciate these men over many weeks. Sargon never wielded his authority unnecessarily and remained open to the arguments of his followers. During their journey, Semiramis had even seen the king accept suggestions put forward by regular soldiers, if they made sense. But when he made a decision, it was never contradicted. How different from her own court. Nineveh's governor Samše had almost driven Semiramis mad with her constant opposition. At the same time, the city elders and the officers in her military were careful not to be too direct about their opinions. Protest came quietly and late, when orders were carried out only poorly or not at all because the leaders were not convinced of their necessity. *Senezon's stubborn opposition to Sargon has its good points*, Semiramis thought approvingly.

The king's plan was simple. While the troops continued their march along the road to the temple, an advance party would cross the herders' rise to reach the east side of the plateau and would wait there until the approaching troops drew the attention of Addad and the muskil at the gates. With a swift advance, they would then enter the temple to confront Addad. Once the thunder god was defeated, the muskil would quickly yield.

Simple as the plan was, success depended on them actually remaining unseen as they climbed. Senezon could not believe that their ascent in the east would go unnoticed by the centaurs. "The muskil must have wondered who drove the goats onto that rise," he said. "The dogs didn't do it by themselves."

"The herdsmen could certainly have made the road to the west without being seen from the temple," Sanherib replied. "The plateau is said to be wide and there must be bushes and trees a man could hide behind. The muskil have no time to search everything, not while they're preparing their defences for our troops. Besides, two simple herdsmen are no threat to Addad."

"Maybe it's something else," Semiramis finally interjected. All eyes turned to the queen. "No human has ever directly challenged a god. Even if we made it undetected and managed to get into the temple, who among us could prevail against Addad?"

Sargon had expected this. The same concern had been on his mind ever since they had left Nineveh, and it had taken him a long time to find an answer. Until that morning.

"A valid objection, Queen Semiramis. But we should keep in mind that Addad is not truly a god. He is the offspring of two helpers created by Ishtar and Marduk. Uras and Anum were powerful, certainly, but neither could stand up to either Ishtar or Marduk. Even Addad does not wield that kind of power."

"Nevertheless, he is stronger than all of the muskil, and stronger than any advance party we can send. He will finish us off easily."

"Unless we can bring an equal opponent with us." With that, the king pulled aside a curtain that covered a branch of the cave. An eerie hiss and the scrape of claws on rock made all present freeze. The mušḫuššu, sinister serpent-dragon of the sun god, thrust its horned head out of the chamber. Semiramis shuddered reflexively at the sight of the fabled creature, and as it crept slowly out towards her, the queen could almost physically feel the uncanny power emanating from it. Its serpentine head towered high above their own, and its watchful eyes took in every movement in the cave.

All but Sargon backed away. He remained in his place, within arm's reach of the creature's scaly body. "Addad planned to divert suspicion onto Marduk's troops with his treacherous attack," he said. "Our God has not forgotten this. He will give the mušḫuššu the strength to face the traitor, while we deal with the muskil." With a hiss, the mušḫuššu seemed to confirm the king's words.

They had one final meeting before setting of the next morning. The king and queen, with Nintinugga and Sanherib, would take the secret ascent to the east. They would be joined by the mušḫuššu and Sargon's bodyguard, as well as a unit of archers from Nineveh. The army would continue along the road to the thunder-god's palace under the command of Senezon, Ezira and Woranola. A disguised chariot with the royal insignia would make an observer think that Semiramis and Sargon were leading their troops from there.

"Approach the walls to within range of the siege weapons, no closer," the king instructed his officers. "Do not expose the troops to their archers. Your task is to distract Addad, not to storm the walls."

Senezon was not happy with this arrangement at all. "And if they attack us? Can we at least fight them hand-to-hand then?"

"You'll get your chance to bash heads in," the king reassured him. "When we've succeeded against Addad, Nintinugga will send one of her singing arrows over the wall. That will be your signal to storm the castle. But not a moment before," he added, looking sternly at his general. Senezon nodded grimly.

After the gathering had dispersed, the king took Ezira aside. The elderly šagana had not said a word during the meeting and seemed to be pursuing his own thoughts.

"What's on your mind, old friend?" the king asked his long-time confidant. "What have we overlooked?" Ezira smiled slightly. It was impossible to hide his thoughts from the king.

"Do you really think Addad will let us reach his walls unscathed? The mountains are his realm. He knows the area well, while we find something new behind every bend in the road. We are far more vulnerable on these steep hillsides than on the plain outside his walls."

"There were several places in the last few days that would have made an excellent ambush," the king said after a moment. "But nothing came, which makes me think that Addad no longer has the troops to face us outside the protection of his walls."

Ezira nodded. "That would be one explanation. But it could also be that we are yet to pass by places even more suitable for an ambush."

"True enough," Sargon had to agree. "So you should be ready for an attack at any moment. The scouts will need to be especially vigilant from now on."

"We should rearrange the units, too," Ezira advised. "Right now, Woranola's catapults are at the tail of our column. If Addad strikes there when we are in a ravine, we will not be able to come to their aid in time."

In Addad's place, Sargon thought, he would do just that. He said: "You're right. Without the siege weapons we would be forced to storm the walls ourselves . . ."

"Which is exactly what I would hope for if I were Addad," Ezira finished the thought.
Grimly, the king nodded. "Let's have a word with Woranola before you leave. Mixing the divisions on a march might break tradition, but she will see the advantage."

Satisfied, Sargon thought back to the subsequent conversation with the gal-ug of Nineveh's long-range weapons. She was used to bringing up the rear of a column, hauling her heavy wagons along the trampled paths and through the dung left by the horses ahead. Now, however, her unit would be at the centre of the force, around which the other units were to arrange themselves as a defensive shell. Her gratitude for the protective buffer offered to her units was not lost on Sargon. *There are good people here in Subartu*, he thought. *Addad's treachery has marked them, but this common threat will help us emerge from the shadows of our past. Together, we will achieve things we would never have believed we were capable of.*

The group around the king and queen had set off early and soon reached the rock face where the herdsmen had come down. Nintinugga grew more and more restless as they approached the mountain. The rock looked vaguely familiar to her, and then all at once she knew where she had seen it before: it was the mountain from which she had fallen so often in her nightmares. In that moment of recognition, her legs almost failed her. In her dreams, the dark rocks and pale ground in the valley had always risen at her when she'd fallen. Had she seen her own future in her sleep? She held tightly to Sanherib's arm.

He knew about her nightmares and seemed to guess her thoughts. "Don't be afraid. I'll hold onto you," he said.

She was grateful for his reassurance, but not convinced. *Marduk, Lord*, she prayed silently. *Were the dreams a warning? Were you telling me you don't want me to go up there?* She looked to her king. Sargon would surely let her take the road with the rest of the army—she only had to ask. But if she did that, she would be leaving him to his fate. If anything were to happen to him, it would be her fault. *Marduk could not want that.* The thought renewed her courage—yes, this was how it had to be. Her nightmare was no more than a test of her loyalty.

Marduk wanted her there to protect her king, and she would not fail him. She threw herself into the climb with renewed energy.

The two herdsmen led the way up the hillside, which quickly grew steep. They were followed by the mušḫuššu, which was evidently used to climbing, the serpent-dragon moving deftly from crevice to crevice. The first time they saw the monster, the herders had jumped up in terror and taken refuge behind a boulder. It took Semiramis some persuasion to convince them that they were in no danger from the creature, but their doubts were not entirely dispelled. The serpent-dragon was apparently not very fond of the herders, either. It kept a little distance behind them—and at the same time, its massive presence urged the two unsettled men to hurry.

Halfway through the day, they reached a plateau large enough to accommodate them all, and Sargon called for a rest. They sat in small groups while the mušḫuššu kept watch at the edge of the plateau. Semiramis sat beneath an overhang that offered some protection from the sun, now high overhead. Sargon came and sat with her. As she had done throughout the long journey, she wore a heavy cloak to protect herself from the sun's rays.

"I will never understand what you Akkadians like about this heat, Sargon," she said. She did not sound morose, however, but rather somewhat amused. "Don't you see how the sun scorches your skin to leather?"

He shrugged. "I suspect that happened so long ago that today we would need a great deal of sun to feel anything at all."

She thought for a moment. "Then the time you spent living under Addad's clouds must have been stifling."

Sargon nodded. "It was a special moment for me when we entered your realm and rediscovered Marduk's radiance. I felt as if our god had been waiting for us in the land of our enemies. We were in a foreign place, and yet the sight of the sun shining in the blue sky was so very familiar. Do you know what I mean?"

She pushed the veil that covered her face a little aside and Sargon looked into her deep blue eyes. "I understand you only too well," she said. "In your kingdom I spent many hours at night in silent conference with Ishtar, and all the while her moon gazed down on me graciously. I had not felt as close to her as I did on those nights for a very long time. I have often asked her why we should abhor a land that she herself bathes in such beautiful light. It does not make sense."

They sat in silence for a while, each pondering the thought. Finally Sargon asked, "Have we misunderstood our gods? They're competing for the sky above us, after all. Where one is, the other cannot be. As their servants, we have to follow as they lead. Otherwise the world has no meaning."

"Yes, we have to follow them. You are right about that. But do you really believe that Marduk's intent is directed against a land over which he spreads his light and where he sends the man closest to him?"

Sargon himself had been plagued by similar thoughts for weeks, and now she was putting them into words. The appearance of the mušḫuššu had finally shaken his concept of the world. If Marduk protected those against whom Sargon had sent his troops for many years, then the king had misread his god's desire. The significance of his conclusion brought a smile to his lips.

"The priests will certainly be surprised by our interpretation, won't they?" he said. "But changing their thinking will take a very long time."

Semiramis, beneath her veil, also smiled. "We saw the first example for ourselves in Nineveh. For my part, I am confident. Ishtar has always embodied love for one another. Peace between our peoples will also open more space for love."

Sargon nodded. "And if grievances are tackled in time and not just complained about, even someone like Senezon will find a way to live well with it."

"Him especially," the queen agreed, and they sat and enjoyed their musings about a peaceful future. Then the mušḫuššu approached. It was time for the final climb to Addad's temple—time to do battle with the thunder god.

The rock face grew steeper and steeper until, finally, they were climbing almost vertically up the mountain. The high sun blinded them as they tried to make out the summit. By now, the herders had gotten used to having the serpent-dragon close behind them and eagerly climbed ahead. Sargon wondered more than once at how sure of their way up the mountain they were. The herdsmen seemed not only used to climbing, but also to have memorised the route perfectly. Sargon had expected that they would stray from the path occasionally and have to reorient themselves, but so far they had climbed steadily and without fail.

After a while, the rock formed an overhang high above them. It was impossible to go any further. On a ledge, the guides stopped and waited those behind them. Some distance away, the mušḫuššu had anchored itself to the rock face with its claws. Its mighty head seemed to be examining the craggy surface.

"Are we on the right track?" the king asked the herders. "There doesn't seem to be any way on from here."

The taller man said, "It's not far now, sire. The overhang stops anyone above from seeing us coming up."

"It looks more like it protects the temple from anyone coming this way. Is this really the path you took on the way down?" he asked, his suspicion growing stronger.

But the men nodded eagerly. "Don't worry. A little way off to the right is an opening in the overhang. This ledge leads us right to it. Once we reach the cave, it's only a few more steps. At the top end of the cave is the plateau and the temple."

"Then lead us to the cave!" the king ordered. He followed close behind the herdsmen, while the mušḫuššu clambered safely along the rock above their heads. The serpent-dragon seemed untroubled by the slippery walls and dizzying heights.

And, in fact, they soon reached a place where the overhang afforded a narrow gap through which they could climb higher. The ascent was a little easier here, but a new problem arose. The gap was too small for the mušḫuššu to pass through. Sargon looked helplessly along the rock, hoping to spot another gap. The serpent-dragon, also recognising the obstacle, was exploring the rock face further away from the group. The guides waited while their companions paused uncertainly.

Semiramis, also aware of the situation, joined Sargon. "Is this the way you came down? Is there another way to get from here up to the temple?" she asked the herdsmen.

The two men looked at each other uncertainly. "We don't know, Your Majesty. We were running away. All we could think of was getting away from the danger. We felt safe in the cave. It was too narrow for the muskil to follow us down here."

"You should have told us about the cave before we started to climb. The mušḫuššu could have looked for another way."

"It can still do that," Sargon broke in. "The mušḫuššu is far more sure-footed here in the mountains than we are. It will find another way up fast enough while we go through the cave." The dragon snarled over at them as if in confirmation. Then it continued its traverse of the rock face—Sargon couldn't help thinking of Senezon, just then leading the army up the path. The axeman would have reacted the same way.

The ascent through the cave proved to be easier than the climb to reach it. Sanherib, who stayed close to Nintinugga, was grateful there was no sun in there to blind him. There were also more places that offered a secure foothold. Soon they could see the exit above them. They were nearing their destination, and he felt his heart beat faster. The group had become quiet. Before they had reached the cave, they had kept their spirits up with songs and shouts. Now, everyone climbed in silence.

Sanherib prepared himself mentally for what lay ahead. The muskil were physically far superior, as he'd discovered first-hand in Mari. But the humans had two advantages: surprise, and the mušḫuššu, once it found a way to rejoin them. He glanced at Nintinugga, who was climbing beside him towards the cave mouth. So far she had handled the climb bravely—Sanherib knew she had revealed her fear of heights to no one but him.

She had kept her eyes ahead, courageously ignoring the abyss behind her. Should he have pushed her to take the road with the army? She answered his unspoken question by kissing his hand and giving him a broad smile. A warmth rose inside him, overcoming his fears for the young woman who had captured his heart. Sanherib shook his head vigorously. He needed to focus on the task ahead. In front of him, his queen was going into battle—and he had sworn to protect her, no matter what.

Already the herders were leading the small group out of the mouth of the cave and into the open. Sargon was with them, his sword already drawn. Large boulders hid their view of the temple, but the king cautiously edged around them until he had a clear view of the stony plateau and the temple itself.

The mountaintop was vast and level, just as the herdsmen had described it. They were crouching beside him now, waiting for his instructions. The temple of the thunder god had been constructed as a stepped temple on three broad terraces, like the ones Sargon had seen in Nineveh. This one, however, loomed far higher than any he'd seen. Indeed, he'd never before seen such a lofty structure. The first level itself was higher than any of the towers in the city. Behind the battlements on the uppermost level was a gleaming white sanctuary, but from where he stood Sargon could only see the back of it, and no way to climb up. As in Nineveh, the processional way to Addad's temple came from the east, with a wide staircase for the processions and two narrower beside it. Opposite these stairs was the fortress gate, where the rest of their troops would soon attack.

In the sky above the temple, dark clouds were piling up into mountains, which Addad would soon send out over the land. In the distance, Sargon saw movement at the fortifications around the gate that opened to the road. A few bushes and boulders and a couple of broken-down wagons were scattered across the plain, but he could see no trees, nor any buildings other than the temple.

It was a peaceful sight. Sargon had expected more animation in a fortress preparing for an attack. The calm that Addad's sanctuary emanated confused him.

"The muskil must be making their preparations inside the temple," Semiramis, who had joined him, reasoned.

"Unless their huts are on the side away from us, facing the gate. That's where I would get them to camp," Sargon replied. He studied the battlements on the lowest level of the structure once more but could see no movement.

He'd seen enough, and returned to rest of the group, still waiting just inside the cave. "The plateau is wider than I thought, but the muskil seem to have all their attention on the road in front of the gates, where they expect us to attack from," he explained. "The battlements at the first level look unguarded. If we can get around to the gate unseen, then we can reach the stairs without being spotted from above. We wait there until our catapults lure the muskil out of their burrows. Then we climb up behind them to the temple at the top and attack Addad."

"Wouldn't it be better to climb the terraces on our side?" asked Nintinugga. "The muskil will never leave the stairs unguarded."

"That was my first thought, too," Sargon said. "But when our troops attack, they won't leave the battlements unguarded either. If we're caught climbing up, we'll be at the mercy of their arrows. All right . . . then shoot your signal arrow for the troops once we reach the temple. We'll need a distraction to get closer to Addad." He turned to their two guides. "We won't need your help from here on. Go home to your families."

Semiramis came to the two herdsmen who had led them this far. They fell on their knees before her. "Take this as a token of my gratitude," she said and handed them a leather pouch.

"Get to safety as fast as you can," Sargon advised. "You know the way." The two men nodded gratefully and turned back into the cave.

Sargon again took the lead, closely followed by Semiramis. From the rocks at the mouth of the cave, he checked again to make sure no one was watching. Then he gave the signal to run, and they ran.

What Sanherib saw ahead of him almost took his breath away. The temple was huge, towering like a mountain before them. From the cave to its base was much further than he'd expected. *The plain is too wide and far too exposed,* he thought grimly. There on the open field, they would be easy targets for enemy arrows. The king, like the other swordsmen, was wearing only light armour, but it would at least offer some protection against arrows. But Semiramis was wearing no armour, only a cloak. A single arrow would kill her. He ran on, wanting to get across the dangerous space as quickly as possible. But as he ran, the impression grew in him more and more that the looming silent walls that increasingly filled his field of vision were watching them.

They had covered about half the distance when the loud clang of metal on metal made him turn. Far behind, Sanherib saw two figures banging shields together and shouting loudly: "Alarm! The enemy is here!" they cried. "They're coming!"

It was the herders who had led them here, he was stunned to see. Their heads held high, they now strode forward, noisily announcing their arrival.

Sargon had also recognised them. "Take cover! It's a trap!" he called. He leapt behind one of the few boulders on the plateau just as first arrows cut the air where he'd been running a moment before.

Nintinugga had also spun around when she heard the noise. She cursed when she saw the traitors. Without thinking about how she herself presented a target to the muskil archers, she nocked an arrow on her bowstring and shot the taller of the two herders dead. Startled, the other man lowered his arms. Nintinugga's second arrow killed him before he could turn to flee. She had no time to celebrate. More and more arrows were now striking the plain near her, too. With a few quick steps, she found cover behind a broken wagon, where Sanherib was already crouching with two swordsmen.

The screams and groans of the injured filled the plain that had previously stretched so peacefully before them. Not everyone had been able to find shelter from the muskil's arrows in time. Nintinugga looked around quickly. About a third of her unit lay injured on the ground. One of the Akkadians was staggering forward, his right leg bleeding badly, an arrow projecting from his calf. A second arrow pierced his shoulder and knocked him to the ground. On his knees, he crawled towards the protection of a rock. Just before he reached it, one of his companions jumped out to help—before they could get to safety, more arrows struck both men down.

High above them, the muskil leader contemplated with satisfaction the predicament of the humans pinned down below. Nizam-Muskil was among the greatest of his race. For many years he had been supreme commander of the temple. He alone was accorded the honour of speaking directly to Addad. Only he knew his master's plan, which had again worked exactly as predicted. *Humans . . . how feeble they are*, the muskil thought with contempt. *They cling so easily to hope and build their future in their minds.* Personally, he would never have believed a story spun by two unknown herders. But humans believe what they want to believe, his master had taught him. That was their weakness. And the humans down there believed they could outwit the mighty Addad and his muskil. Soon they would learn how terribly wrong they were.

A guard trotted up to the muskil leader. "There are about twenty of them still alive," he reported eagerly. "Only five are carrying bows. Should we surround them and finish them off?"

Nizam Muskil shook his head grimly. "Not yet," he said. "Lord Addad has something special in mind for them. Before we extinguish their existence, he wants to punish them personally for their arrogance. The people should never forget the cost of daring to challenge the thunder god." *Nor how futile it is*, he added in thought. He stepped up to the battlements and bellowed down to the humans barricaded below, as Addad had instructed him to do.

"Pathetic worms! How dare you challenge our God! Who are you to think you can threaten him?" Expecting no response and getting none, he continued, "Addad laughs at your wretched endeavours. To him, you are nothing but dust stirred by the wind."

This time, too, there was no answer from below.

"Nothing to say?" the muskil goaded. "I want to hear you wail. Look to the road below, where your brave army crawls. Watch as their end draws near."

At first, the climb was innocuous. *It's too easy,* Senezon thought grimly. As usual, he moved ahead of his troops. He preferred to see for himself their surroundings and to set the pace for the army behind him. There was no need to hurry unnecessarily. The road up to the temple was mostly wide and surprisingly well surfaced. Even the heavy wagons with the catapults made good progress. Nevertheless, Senezon's mood was bleak. "It's just too easy," he thought again, this time muttering the words aloud.

"You think so?" asked Ezira, striding beside him. His old friend was a picture of calm.

Senezon, surly, growled, "I was talking to myself, not you."

Ezira let out a throaty laugh. "You've said it so many times that I thought you might finally want someone to answer you."

"It's true, though," the axeman defended himself. "I feel like a pig on a platter, ready for slaughter before a banquet. All the guests are staring at you, licking their chops and thinking which piece of you they're going to cut off."

"You have strange thoughts," his friend replied. "I didn't know you had such . . . moments of empathy before dinner. You're usually the first to get his hands on a drumstick."

"But don't you feel like we're being watched, too?" Senezon countered, offended. "It's like a thousand eyes are on us. What are they waiting for? We passed one place this morning . . . Addad couldn't have wished for better. And nothing happened. Again. This waiting is driving me crazy."

He would have preferred any skirmish to being forced to wait like this. Had they whipped Addad's army so badly that they could not even strike back when the odds were on their side?

They had reached a place where the road had narrowed and was barely wider than the wagons. Stones had crumbled dangerously from under the wheels as the heavy catapults rolled over them. They needed every hand to secure the horses and stop them from breaking free. The entire time, directly above them, a tongue of rock hung menacingly. From below, they could not have seen anything lurking up there—a single troop of archers could have created a bloodbath among them. But the attack did not come, and the army passed the danger point unscathed. The war of nerves continued.

If your enemy doesn't attack, it doesn't mean he can't, Senezon reminded himself.

Ezira seemed to share his concerns. "In his place, you or I would have taken the opportunity. But we don't know how Addad thinks or what his plans are. He's a god, after all. And who knows the thoughts of a god?"

"Thank you. That really eases my mind," his friend grumbled grimly. "If he doesn't show his face soon, I'm more likely to die of old age than from an axe wound."

"Let's hope you live that long," Ezira murmured.

Hofileshgu kept close to her wagons during the procession. She kept pacing back and forth, keeping constant watch over her precious weapons. They had only two of the big catapults with them, and they had to be brought into position at all costs if the desert king's plan was to succeed. The men and women in her units were holding up admirably. They were not used to travelling far from the city, but they remained alert and were disciplined in their work. She was grateful that Sargon had ordered the guns to be moved to the centre of the column and not left at the tail.

Hofileshgu was in awe of the high mountain walls surrounding them. She imagined the devastating effect one of her catapults could have if it were mounted above the road to fire on an army marching below, as they were doing. *It would be shooting practice*, she thought uneasily. The catapults would be out of range of any arrows and could take all the time they needed to aim. She wouldn't even have to hit the troops—she would only have to damage the road enough for the troops to be pinned down. Like Senezon, she was growing more and more restless the longer the day went on without an attack.

Woranola had divided her archers into two squads, one marching immediately in front of the catapult wagons and one behind. She herself stayed with the second group, the only officer among them. Should the enemy surround them, her archers would entrench themselves on the slopes.

Around midday, the combined army of Subartuans and Akkadians stopped to rest. The scouts estimated that they could cover the remaining distance to the temple in three hours. Senezon had the equipment checked and drummed into his soldiers that they should expect an attack at any moment. The path became a little steeper from where they stopped to rest, but the road was still good. Ezira guessed that Addad had had his siege engines built in the temple for the attack on Nineveh and had then had to fortify the roads to carry them. But that didn't take away the sinking feeling in Senezon's gut that the well-paved roads were leading them into a trap.

Around a bend in the road, they had a view of a high plateau capped by the three-tiered temple of the thunder god. They were seeing it from the east, and no walls blocked their view—the mountainsides here were extremely steep, and no wall was required. Senezon held a hand over his eyes, shielding them from the glare as he peered upwards. He could make out no movement. The king should have reached the top with the mušḫuššu and the advance party by now if the herdsmen had kept their word. *Far too many "ifs" in our plan*, he thought. He lowered his gaze again, looking forward to where the road butted up against a rock face in a long straight line. Ahead, he could already see the bend where Hofileshgu would set up her catapults, and where their exposed and nervous march would finally be over. Senezon urged the troops onward.

From the plateau, Semiramis watched as her united army marched along the road in orderly lines. She could not make out individuals, but the tall catapult wagons were clearly visible in their midst. So far, the units seemed to have survived the ascent unharmed.

The approaching troops had not gone unnoticed in the temple. Nizam-Muskil beckoned one of his fighters. "The worms are coming out of their holes," he said. "Time to trample them." The fighter bowed. "Start the with the siege units. We'll split them up and crush them one by one. Let their leaders watch the slow destruction."

The muskil nodded. He trotted along the battlements and down the temple stairs. At the bottom, he was met by two more muskil. All three carried long sturdy poles.

Together, they galloped towards a row of rocks already piled at the edge of the slope many months before. The small group of humans taking cover nearby did not concern them. The muskil archers were watching the plateau from the temple. If the humans dared to interfere, they would quickly die. Powerless, all they could do was watch.

From above, Nizam-Muskil looked down with satisfaction as his fighters snapped the trap shut. When the three muskil reached the piled rocks, they moved their poles into position behind them.

Semiramis was the first to realise Addad's evil plan. "The rocks, Sargon!" she cried. "They don't need troops at all. They've got enough rocks there to finish the entire army."

Sargon, also realising what was about to happen, formed his hands into a funnel and bellowed with all his might, "Back! You're walking into a trap. Run for your lives!" But the only answer he got was from the scornful wind, which blew the king's words back in his face. Try as he might, his voice did not reach beyond the plateau.

The others, too, began shouting frantically to warn their unsuspecting comrades on the road. *The singing begins,* Nizam Muskil thought cruelly. *Save your voices, worms. They can't hear you and you'll have more than enough opportunities to scream today.*

The muskil at the rocks heard their desperate shouts, too. Their leader turned and waved grimly at Sargon, like a fighter in the arena before giving his opponent the coup de grâce. Then with all his might he leaned on the end of the long wooden pole he'd already jammed under a boulder. The boulder crunched and started to rise. Another pole was pushed into the gap that appeared underneath it, moving the boulder a little higher. The grating of rock on rock grew louder. The third pole joined in, levering the boulder slowly out of its bed. The muskil were sweating with the strain as it rolled to the edge of the precipice . . . and over, crashing onto the slope below and taking more and more rocks with it. Tremors and the growl of the tumbling rocks shook the plateau.

Now the soldiers on the road saw the danger from above. Semiramis saw the orderly ranks of her troops dissolve as they scrambled to get to safety. Then swirling dust swallowed the sight, but cruel Addad's wind still carried the unearthly crashing of the rocks onto the road and the screams of her people up to her. *What were we thinking*, she despaired. *We are just toys to Addad, to toss around as he pleases*. The queen strained to see the road through the dust. Had anyone survived?

Ezira, at the head of the column, was the first to see the tumbling rocks.

"Run!" he shouted to the soldiers. "As fast as you can!" And already he was hurrying up the road.

Woranola also raised her head reflexively when she heard the noise high above, and she looked up in horror at the rocks hurtling down the mountain.

"Rockfall! Leave the wagons!" she yelled. She ordered her rearguard troops back the way they'd come to avoid the masses of rock. There was chaos on the road as soldiers tried to squeeze past the supply wagons, panicking and shouting as they pushed and shoved each other to get out of the path of the rocks.

Hofileshgu, meanwhile, found herself caught between the two wagons that held the catapults, but immediately recognized the danger that threatened the catapults: trapped between the heavy wagons and the long lines of soldiers, there was no way out for them.

But even in her desperation, she kept the clear head that her soldiers had always admired. Coolly, she calculated the path of the falling rocks and saw that they would strike just behind her. Amidst the chaos, she tried to stay calm and determined.

"Leave the third wagon. Join up with us, forward. Keep the front wagons moving. Try not to run but keep moving." The men and women heard the order and the calm confidence in her voice. In the mass of shouting, frantic soldiers, they carried out the order silently and pushed forward even as the rocks crashed louder and louder.

With a tremendous leap, the first boulder slammed into the rear catapult, sending splintered timbers flying at people and animals alike and leaving them screaming on the ground. More rocks smashed onto the road, which disintegrated under their feet and tumbled down the slope. More and more boulders rained down, and the flying dust mixed with blood, screams, and wails.

When the rockfall finally stopped, Hofileshgu dared to look back for the first time. Where the second wagon had been, the road had vanished, carried away down the slope. A crevasse that could easily have held two wagons now gaped between her and the rearguard under Woranola's command. *Did she survive?* Hofileshgu wondered. But the injured on her side of the crevasse were the more pressing issue. "Take care of them," she instructed her platoon leaders. "We're not leaving anyone behind here." One by one, the injured were lifted onto the wagons.

Far above, Nizam-Muskil studied the results of the first strike with satisfaction. His soldiers had already moved to the second boulder, intended to cut off the leading troops, and had set their poles in place. With a face like stone, he gave the signal.

Senezon was running up the road. He was breathing hard, trying to keep up with Ezira. He had not expected the old spearman to have the stamina he was now showing. In the thin air and with the weight of his axe, Senezon was struggling more and more. From behind, the screams of the fallen still rang in his ears, but he found no time to turn around. Then he heard again the fateful crunch and crash of boulders from above. He looked up desperately towards the temple, from where more rocks were breaking loose. This time they were tumbling directly at him.

"Back!" he bellowed in horror. "The rocks!" His troops came to a halt instantly as the masses of rock thundered down above them. It was impossible to get up far enough up the road in time. Senezon turned his soldiers back down the road even as the first rocks crashed into it, obliterating it instantly and sweeping it down the mountain. Their route to the temple was cut off. They were trapped.

Twenty-Fourth Chapter:
Twilight of the Gods

From where he was sheltering behind the rock, Sargon could only watch helplessly as his army was being wiped out on the narrow mountain road. The muskil were already working on the remaining rocks, which would soon come crashing down on those trapped below.

Far above them, dark clouds were gathering over the temple. The wind grew stronger and stronger, howling an eerie death-song. Lightning flashed across the sky, followed by thunder that made the rocks quake. In the tumult, Sargon saw a huge human-like figure appear atop the temple. Horns sprouted from its mighty head, and powerful arms hurled bolts of lightning into the sky.

Addad, the god of thunder.

Beside Sargon, Semiramis had also watched the spectacle silently. Her face had turned pale, but her lips were pressed together resolutely. The thunder god had materialised in person to show the people the futility of their deeds in their moment of annihilation. "We have to buy our troops time to get off the road," she said firmly to Sargon. "There are only three of them at the rocks, and twenty of us."

"Eighteen," Sargon corrected her. "And you're forgetting the archers on the battlements. There's no cover between here and the rocks. The moment we run, they can pick their targets. We won't get through."

"There is a way," Semiramis said, and something in her voice told Sargon that the queen had made a momentous decision. "Nintinugga's arrows will carry as far as the muskil on the battlements. Once those two are down, our group will be able to reach the rocks before the muskil can get reinforcements."

"Ninti would be dead before she even drew back her bowstring," Sargon said. "You've seen yourself how quickly the muskil can find their target. Time is too short."

"Not if the archers have a more attractive target," the queen replied.

Sargon guessed with horror what Semiramis had in mind. "It's suicide. You're not wearing armour. One arrow would kill you!"

"And I suppose I will not die if we keep sitting here? Addad has all the time in the world while our troops are slain and we are pinned down here."

Sargon protested. He did not want her to waste her life senselessly. She saw the concern in his face and smiled at him gratefully.

"I am touched at your regard for my life, Sargon, King of Akkad." She sounded very formal now, although she addressed him by name. "I was not mistaken in you. You protect your people, but you are not indifferent to the people of my realm either." She took a clay tablet from a pocket of her robe and handed it to him.

"When I am gone, give this to the high priestess. She will give you a casket with instructions for my people.

The first is for my daughter, Ataliya. She is to be your consort, so that you may rule together and make peace between our peoples."

Sargon was speechless. He stared at the tablet Semiramis had pressed into his hand. Beside her seal was a brief directive for the high priestess to carry out what she had already been told. There were no explanations or conditions—Semiramis had evidently prepared the high priestess for such a possibility before they had left Nineveh. He tried once more to dissuade her from her desperate plan. "There must be another way. Your people need you. Addad cannot triumph over us like this."

"And he won't, as long as we don't let him drive a wedge between us again. It has been a wonderful journey with you, Sargon. I would not have wanted to miss any of the moments we shared. We owe you our thanks for saving Nineveh. My death is the least I can give in return."

But Sargon would not be convinced. "No," he grated through clenched teeth. "I won't let you go like this."

A thunderous roar made him spin around. Another lethal volley of rocks hurtled down the steep slope at the helpless troops. The thudding impact and screams rang back up to them as the chunks of stone found their target. Semiramis looked intently at Sargon.

"Sargon! How many more have to die? It is our last chance."

Finally, he relented. "So be it. Queen Semiramis, it has been my honour to serve you in Nineveh."

She said nothing but pulled him close and kissed him firmly on the lips. He was too astonished to try to stop her.

Then she turned and shouted to the archer from Akkad. "Nintinugga! There are two muskil up there, one at each corner of the first level. You can reach them with Kalbaba's bow. We will distract them and give you the time you need. Remember what you have learned about the bow. It will save you and your king." Turning to Sargon, she said, "Thank you, Sargon. Thank you for your trust and for the past weeks in your company. Now grant me a final wish. I want Ishtar to see her daughter when she goes to her death for you. Marduk will not close his mind to this, not if it is *you* who ask him."

Sargon, as if enchanted, still felt the pressure of her lips on his. But his resistance to her plan was broken. He knelt in prayer, aligning his body with the sun, which glowed red-hot on the horizon. Memories crept up from deep his mind. How often had he prayed to his god when day gave way to night? As a child, he had prayed for Marduk to dispel the fearsome darkness of night, but the darkness had always returned and stayed until its power failed. Things were different now. For Sargon, the night had lost its menace. Now he knew the other side, and how it promised peace to the dazzled eye and cooled sunburned skin. Semiramis had opened his eyes to another world that belonged just as much to humankind. The night in Subartu was her realm. It was only right that she should depart this place as queen, in plain view of her goddess.

Sargon knelt and forced his mind towards prayer. The moments he had spent in Subartu flashed before his inner eye. There had been happy nights, sitting and joking with Gusur and Senezon at the tent outside Nineveh. Then he thought of their triumph and how they had repulsed the muskil before the city walls. In all those moments, Ishtar had graciously allowed her celestial light to shine over them. Now Sargon asked his own god, Marduk, to grant Ishtar admission to his kingdom of the day, so that she might behold her daughter's valiant deed. Deeper and deeper the king pushed down into his prayer, until he was so deep that he hardly heard the astonished cries of his troops when the disc of the moon emerged between two peaks in the far east. Ishtar rose into her realm in the face of Marduk's sun.

Behind the wagon, Nintinugga and Sanherib watched the spectacle in silence. Gently, thoughtfully, Nintinugga placed one hand on his.

Soon the moonlight had reached the plateau and reflected from Semiramis's cloak, which shimmered in every fold. Her hair glowed silver. It was as if a second moon had risen next to Sargon. The king marvelled at the sight. The queen stood tall, her gaze fixed on the distant moon of her goddess, determined to fulfil her last mission.

"It is time," she whispered and strode to the edge of the boulder behind which they had found shelter from the arrows. Sargon prepared to charge the muskil.

Just then, he heard the throaty snarl of a wild animal. A lion, magnificently maned, had appeared behind them, emerging from the cave that had led them onto the plateau. Others followed, roaring as they ran past the trapped soldiers and on towards the temple. Ishtar herself had joined the fight.

On the battlements, Nizam-Muskil was suddenly nervous. Where had the lions come from? His archers reacted immediately and began firing at these unwanted newcomers. But however good their aim, it wasn't enough. More and more lions ran from the cave. Then Nizam-Muskil heard a menacing hiss behind him. He wheeled around and found himself face to face with

the serpentine head of the mušḫuššu. His warning cry
was cut short as a stab of its scorpion tail hurled him
over the battlements. The serpent-dragon, after a long
climb, had reached the plateau from the north side and
had climbed to the battlements unobserved. Now it
rushed at the archers, as surprised as Nizam-Muskil had
been, and who could only stare at the serpent-dragon.
Distracted, unmoving, they became an easy target for
Nintinugga's whistling arrows. They were dead before
the mušḫuššu reached them.

At the same time, a majestic white lion with a long
mane appeared in the mouth of the cave. It studied
the battle on the plateau and then padded to the rock
behind which Semiramis and Sargon still sheltered.
Semiramis recognised in the beast her goddess's heraldic animal, and she went down on her knees before it.
Sargon stood and stared at the lion in amazement. He
was a child of the desert, where an encounter with a
lions usually ended fatally. Experience had taught him
to gauge who would emerge victorious if it came to a
fight. The mass of the animal told him that it was far
superior to any human. The lion stepped closer slowly
until it reached the kneeling queen. With a shake of
its magnificent mane, it commanded her to stand. The
queen placed a grateful hand on the animal's neck.

The falling muskil's scream made Sargon look up.
He saw the huge body fall and only then noticed the
fight on the battlements. The lion in front of him let out
a triumphant roar.

"The mušḫuššu is on the battlements!" shouted Sargon to his companions. "To the rocks!" And already he
was running across the plateau.

Nintinugga and Sanherib were instantly running
with him. The muskil at the rocks, realising that some-

thing had happened, turned in horror to see Ishtar's white lions running at them. At first, they used their long poles to keep the animals at bay, but they could not hold back the attackers' superior numbers forever. Nintinugga killed one of them with a long shot from her bow, and the lions pounced on the other two.

By the time the humans reached the rocks, the lions were already rushing on to attack the remaining musk-il. Sargon ordered five of his men to guard the rocks. He didn't want to risk anyone coming from behind and using the terrible weapon against the army trapped below. Then he and Semiramis followed the great lion to the long main staircase that led to the sanctuary atop the temple.

Up at the second terrace, the staircase led into a temple-like portico. From below, the humans could already hear the sounds of battle from inside. They rushed up the steps two and three at a time while the lions loped ahead, tearing down anyone who stood in their way. The bloodied bodies of muskil and lions marked their path, and inside the portico the found more dead musk-il and the remains of several lions.

Addad seemed to have no followers left except the loyal centaurs from Lake Urmia. Terrible as their weapons were, they were no match for the combined onslaught of the gods. At the end of the hall was a magnificent staircase. Sargon was in time to see the mušhuššu bring down a huge muskil with a sweep of its tail, while beside him the massive lion tore another guard to the floor. Their path to the stairs was clear. They hurried past statues of Addad and several sacrificial altars to the stairs and followed the agile lion and mušhuššu upwards. The second staircase was almost as long as the first, and halfway up it led back to the outside of the structure. Still far above them, the white sanctuary glowed. Behind it billowed ominous storm clouds alive with lightning.

"The stairway to the gods," Semiramis said devoutly. "Addad is up there."

"Then we shouldn't keep him waiting!" cried Nintinugga exuberantly. Running with the lions had energised her—for her, now, nothing seemed impossible. The king, however, was more cautious.

"The gods have already gone ahead of us, Ninti. Remember that we are only here as their helpers, so let's see what we can do to help them when they face Addad."

With that he set off, following the stairway out of the building and back into the open. As he climbed, he kept a close eye on their surroundings. The others followed him. The mušḫuššu and the lion had already reached the top—he could no longer see them from the stairs.

Outside it was almost completely dark. The sun had disappeared behind the hills and the moon was swathed in heavy clouds, Addad again blocking all sight of the stars. The wind on the plateau had turned into a storm that howled and tugged at their clothes. Sargon tried to shout something to his companions, but his voice could not overcome the storm even at such close range. He continued to climb. There was still no movement from the sanctuary high above. Then hail began to fall, heavy grains beating down on them like flung pebbles. From one moment to the next, the ice turned the steps into a slippery slope.

They had to lean close to the stairs, with the storm threatening to pick them up and blow them away bodily. With each step they took, it blew harder, and the hail stung their faces. Nintinugga had her bow strapped to her back and was using both hands for support as she climbed. Grimly, the storm whipping at his long hair, Sargon turned and looked back at his companions. Semiramis was just behind him, with the others following bravely after her. The queen was struggling against the gale, the light fabric of her cloak swirling and tugging at her, threatening to throw her off balance. But she kept low and did not stop. She knew Sanherib was close behind to support her if she lost her footing.

Exhausted and soaked, Sargon finally reached the top of the stairway. The white sanctuary rose high in front of him. Torches lit the interior brightly, casting their shine out onto the open space outside. Smoke filled the entire hall, and within it he saw large shadows in battle and heard supernatural screams mixed with a hard, snake-like hiss.

The humans passed cautiously through the mighty sanctuary doors and approached the battle of the gods. Inside, the air was stuffy, hot, and hard to breathe. The howling of the storm outside was now eclipsed by the battle of the rivals inside. The mušḫuššu emerged from the smoke and disappeared back into it with a leap. Sargon could make out a large shadow in the middle, roughly human in shape but more than twice as tall, with horns curving over long hair. A huge double-bladed axe swung menacingly through the smoke. Lightning flashed, and enraged cries rang out when it found its target.

Nintinugga stepped a little to one side and nocked an arrow to her bowstring. When she saw an opening, she let it fly. The familiar whistle rang momentarily as her arrow disappeared in the smoke—then an angry grunt came as it found its target. A huge hand appeared from the cloud and hurled a flashing spear at the spot from which the attack had come. Instinctively, Nintinugga had already changed position—which saved her life. The lightning struck the pillar where she'd been standing just a moment before. The stone shattered and the pillar toppled forward. Nintinugga let out a startled scream as the roof above her collapsed. Beams and tiles came crashing down on. Her companions were safe in another corner of the hall, but Nintinugga was buried beneath a pile of stones and dust.

Sanherib cried out when she disappeared. He began to dig frantically into the rubble. Semiramis came to his aid and helped him clear the debris.

The storm had returned now, too, the hail beating down on them through the now-open roof. Another flash of lightning from the dust cloud destroyed the pillar behind Sargon. The Akkadian saw the ceiling above him disintegrating and leapt clear of the falling stones. He sheathed his sword and went to help the queen and Sanherib.

In front of them, the battle of the gods raged with undiminished ferocity. A sliver of wood had embedded itself in Sanherib's left shoulder. Blood streamed from the wound and stained the stones red. He ignored it. He kept digging into the rubble, lifting aside stone after stone. As he hauled aside a beam, a familiar hand reached up to him from a hollow between two large chunks of stone.

"Nothing happened to the bow," were the first words that came from the pit. Sanherib could not hold back his tears—Ninti was alive. Together, he and Semiramis helped her back to her feet.

Sargon, meanwhile, returned his attention to their opponent and the battle between the gods. Neither side seemed to have the upper hand. Addad kept Ishtar's and Marduk's two helpers at a distance while they were able to stop him from counterattacking. Their fight looked like it could go on forever.

"If we're going to help our gods to victory, we have to do our part," Sargon said to Semiramis. "Even if it means our own death," he added, glancing at Sanherib and Nintinugga. "I say we circle Addad to divide his attention. On my signal, we throw our weapons at the same time. It won't matter where we hit him as long as we distract him and give the gods a chance to strike him down."

They looked from one to the other and nodded. Nintinugga gave Sanherib a fleeting kiss on the lips and then took up position. Sargon strode around to the opposite side of the chamber. Semiramis and Sanherib positioned themselves in front of what had once formed the doorway to the sanctuary. He raised his spear, and the queen cradled her throwing knife in one hand. Nintinugga chose a heavy arrow. The distance to the target was short. Her shot would hit the thunder god. Sargon had decided to sacrifice his short sword. If it missed its target, he would be unarmed, but his sword could do little against a god's lightning, anyway.

He wondered if Addad knew their plan. He must have known that they had survived his attack, but no lightning bolts flew at them as they positioned themselves for the final assault. Sargon found a table and climbed onto it—from there he could study the room from a more elevated position. His companions were ready and waiting for his signal. Again and again, powerful shadows moved and darted inside the smoke.

Sargon waited until he could clearly see the thunder god's head. That was his target.

"Now!" he bellowed, and he hurled his sword at Addad with all his might. Nintinugga screamed from the other side as she let her arrow fly, and Semiramis and Sanherib also flung their weapons at the thunder god. Metal clanged metal as Addad swung his mighty double axe protectively—it smashed the humans' puny weapons, even Nintinugga's arrow, as if they were made of straw. The move occupied the thunder god's axe for barely a second, but it was long enough for the mušḫuššu to strike. Its scorpion sting tore a gaping wound in the thunder god's chest. At the same time, the lion leapt at Addad and buried its teeth deep into one of his arms. Addad staggered as the double-edged axe slipped from his grasp. Lightning flashed in all directions. Hail the size of eggs fell from the sky, and thunder made the floor tremble beneath their feet. The thunder god went down on his knees just as a mighty bolt of lightning struck from the sky, bringing the remains of the sanctuary down on top of the fearsome trio of fighters. Sargon again had to leap clear of the falling boulders. With an ear-splitting crash, the battlefield disappeared under stone and rubble, accompanied by mighty, rumbling thunder that rolled through the valleys.

Then silence fell on the mountain. The storm dissolved, taking the hail with it. Slowly, the smoke cleared from the place where the gods had measured themselves. In the darkness Sargon could see no more than a mound of rubble where titanic forces had raged just moments before. There was no trace of Addad or the superhuman beasts. The ruins of the white sanctuary lay before him, silent.

Then Sargon noticed a movement to his left. Semiramis was climbing over the ruins towards him. A broad smile lit up her face. Sanherib hurried across to his companion on the other side—in her mind, Semiramis was already saying goodbye to her faithful protector. A new friend was waiting for her, a man from the once distant but now much closer land to the south.

A gentle wind swept the murky clouds from the face of the moon, and Ishtar, after so many years, again had an undimmed view of her country. Her ivory light shone brightly down on Sargon and Semiramis, and with it peace returned to their realms.

About the Author

Guido Schenk has been working as a manager for international publishing houses and technology companies for over 20 years. His sales activities motivated him to delve deeper into the topic of storytelling. Communicating ideas in the form of stories has always characterised his work with customers and employees. Guido Schenk lives with his wife in Dublin, writes part-time and coaches about storytelling. Lion of Ishtar is his first novel.

Milton Keynes UK
Ingram Content Group UK Ltd.
UKHW010842271023
431440UK00004B/182